# HOBSON'S ISLAND

## Stefan Themerson

PREFACE BY
BARBARA WRIGHT

DALKEY ARCHIVE PRESS

NORMAL · LONDON

First published in the UK by Faber and Faber Ltd., 1988
Copyright © 1988 by Stefan Themerson
Preface copyright © 2005 by Barbara Wright

First U.S. edition, 2005

Library of Congress Cataloging-in-Publication Data available.
ISBN: 1-56478-417-7

Partially funded by a grant from the Illinois Arts Council, a state agency.

Dalkey Archive Press is a nonprofit organization located at Milner Library
(Illinois State University) and distributed in the UK by
Turnaround Publisher Services Ltd. (London).

www.dalkeyarchive.com

Printed on permanent/durable acid-free paper and bound in
the United States of America.

## PRAISE FOR STEFAN THEMERSON

"Themerson's neo-surrealist style enables him felicitously to interweave incongruities, ludic exercises, shrewd observations, jokes, lightly worn learning, *cris de couer* and parables."
—Peter Reading, *Times Literary Supplement*

"When all is said and done, Themerson is in the company of Carroll and Queneau, a master of controlled inconsequence, God's spy with no one to give reports to, a fine flea in the ear of the modern novel."
—Robert Nye, *Guardian*

"Nearly as mad as the world."
—Bertrand Russell

"Ingenious and imaginatively perverse."
—Kenneth Burke, *American Scholar*

"This book is not only a mystery and an entertainment—it is a fascinating puzzle."
—*Christian Science Monitor*

# OTHER WORKS BY STEFAN THEMERSON IN ENGLISH

# PREFACE

Searching for a true description of Polish-born Stefan Themerson for this American edition of *Hobson's Island*, my mind kept returning to a word that isn't in *Webster's* and so must be very British: "One-off." The English dictionary says that, as a noun, it refers to "A unique or remarkable person."

Nothing could be truer than that. But Themerson would have raised his eyebrows at my reference to Poles, Americans, Britons . . . To him, nationalities were an irrelevance: people were people. Even as a child he had his own ideas, and as they evolved into his philosophy of life he expressed them in his books, hoping to encourage people to think for themselves, to question everything they were told. He saw wars, and many of the woes of the world, as being the direct result of preconceived ideas, ideologies, conformism, hierarchies, classifications, nationalism . . .

One of the most "unique and remarkable" things about Themerson's writings is that, given their serious content, they are full of wit and humour. Among his twenty or so books, seven were novels, into which he always smuggled his philosophical ideas. His characters express them clearly and simply, often in the course of casual conversation, never as if they are preaching. They take it that these ideas are common currency among civilized people. If only they were! The characters here, in *Hobson's Island*, his last novel, bring his basic theses to exciting life.

Born in 1910 in a small town on the Vistula, Stefan went for a while to Warsaw University. There he studied physics and architecture, but didn't stay the course. He must have known even as a twenty-year-old that he could educate himself better than any academy could. He gained a knowledge of all the arts, the sciences, the classics, he pondered over ethics, theology, philosophy . . . He became a friend of Bertrand Russell, and exchanged ideas with him in a long and erudite correspondence, which ended only with Russell's death. This too was shot through with humour. Russell praised his 1949 novel *Bayamus* as "nearly as mad as the world," and wrote a preface to his 1953 *Professor Mmaa's Lecture*.

In 1931 he married the painter Franciszka Weinles, the star pupil of the Warsaw Academy of Fine Arts, and when they weren't writing or painting they were sending shockwaves through Poland with the avant-garde films they made together. But they felt they needed to be in touch with a wider culture than could be found in the Poland of the time, and in the winter of 1937 they went to live in Paris. They had only just got established there, though, when the war started: Franciszka went to work for the Polish Government in Exile, and Stefan, paradoxically and against all his principles, immediately joined the Polish Army in France. (They wanted to make him an officer, but when it came to shouting orders to his underlings, he just couldn't. So a private he remained, throughout his service.) When the Nazis invaded France in 1940, his regiment was in Brittany. The Polish officers simply abandoned their men and somehow got themselves whisked over to England, leaving the "other ranks" to do the best they could. Which meant walking aimlessly to what they hoped would be a safer part of France. Stefan managed to make his way to a Red Cross refuge in Voiron, near Grenoble, and Franciszka managed to catch the last boat going from Bayonne to England. For a long time neither knew what had happened to the other, but eventually the Red Cross put them in touch. It wasn't until 1942, though, that Stefan was able to take the Resistance route via Spain and Portugal to freedom in Britain. He had to rejoin his regiment—still as a private—in Scotland, but after a time was able to join Franciszka in London.

Here they made two films for the Polish Ministry of Information and Documentation. By this time Stefan was writing in English, but English publishers were slow to understand his "unique and remarkable" books, so in 1948 he and Franciszka decided to found their own publishing house. They called it the Gaberbocchus Press. They knew that a Victorian parson had translated Lewis Carroll's poem "Jabberwocky" into Latin, and called the strange animal "Gaberbocchus"—but the English didn't know that, and once again were slow—very slow—to appreciate this strange press with the foreign name, run by these strange people and publishing such strange books . . . Now, of course, Gaberbocchus is regarded as one of the most extraordinary and valuable avant-garde publishing houses the English have ever had.

Their list has become valuable in financial terms too, which is ironical, as finding enough money was a problem to the Themersons all their lives. It was the one thing they were no good at—they just couldn't bring themselves to be interested in it. Stefan once told me that at the beginning, they were naïve enough to think that publishing houses made money. Not so: every Gaberbocchus book, however lovingly written (or translated), illustrated, designed, produced, or printed, had to wait until enough money was somehow scraped together. A few friends bought a few shares in the company—that was about it.

I met them not long before they started Gaberboccus, in the years when I was struggling to be a housewife and mother, and, whenever possible, a pianist. It was just casually that they one day asked me whether I would like to translate Alfred Jarry's *Ubu Roi*, and equally casually that I replied something like, "And sure, why shouldn't I?" I was yearning to do something real, something undomestic, which I could do in a domestic situation. So bit-by-bit I translated it, bit-by-bit I submitted my drafts to the Themersons, and gently and kindly, but firmly, I was shown what to do. When I came to the poems at the end of the play and said they couldn't possibly be made to rhyme, they simply told me not to be silly, to go home and come back with them when they did rhyme. So I did. The Themersons taught me to translate, and I am eternally grateful to them.

There was obviously never any possibility of Gaberbocchus's authors being paid, nor did it occur to anyone to bother with a contract. And yet—Time Marches On!—James Laughlin became an energetic admirer of Gaberbocchus and took over several of their books, including some of my translations, for publication in America. Contracts were made. And now, decades later, I *still* receive a welcome check from New Directions every May. Amateur dramatic societies in America, mainly in universities, are *still* staging *Ubu Roi*. But when it first came out in England, the few critics who took notice of it were agreed that nobody could possibly be interested in this old thing anymore. The first edition, though, was one of Franciszka's most brilliant productions. She invented a new technique especially for *Ubu*: the translation was handwritten in thick black ink directly onto lithographic plates, the writing was overlaid by her inimitable illustrations, the whole printed on yellow paper. The first edition of 1,000 copies took ten years to sell. Now, though, if you ever come across one in the catalogue of an antiquarian bookseller, you probably won't be able to afford it.

Gaberbocchus was now publishing Stefan's books as he wrote them, and with a few striking exceptions they met with the same "normal" cool reception from the English critics as had Jarry's *Ubu*. His books were too original, too individual, too different. Gradually, gradually, though, Stefan's different mind began to be appreciated, and just two years before his death Faber & Faber published his novel *The Mystery of the Sardine*, and two years after that, *Hobson's Island*.

Before this, though, in 1981, the University of Leyden had invited him, in the wake of people like Noam Chomsky, Golo Mann, and Mary McCarthy, to give the university's annual Johan Huizinga lecture. Published the following year, his lecture is a summing up of Themerson's wisdom of a lifetime. He called it *The Chair of Decency*, and had the temerity to suggest to this august university that they find such a chair. He confessed that it took courage to advocate something so apparently simple: "Decency! What an embarrassing word! You have to brace yourself to pronounce it . . . People think you are a sissy, a nincompoop." But he told his Dutch audience that he had found support in the historian in honor of whom those lectures were founded, and he quoted Huizinga as saying, "Nowadays . . . in every depiction of reality in either word or image the element of passion must be played up. Moral norms definitely may not be praised. Virtuous people assure themselves of their halo of the modern by means of a eulogy of immorality."

Stefan began his lecture by offering his audience two theses. The first: "Means are of greater importance than aims." The second: "Contrary to what clergymen and policemen want us to believe, gentleness is biological, and aggression is cultural; not vice versa." And he repeats several times his conviction that human survival depends not on ethical *terminology*, but on ethical *behaviour*. "All ideologies, all missions, all aims corrupt . . . Because, when all is said and done, decency of means *is* the aim of aims."

Beliefs—and even good intentions—lead to blind wickedness. (Themerson had a long correspondence with Bertrand Russell about beliefs.)

•

As I have said, the complicated, suspenseful plots of Stefan's novels are based on these convictions, and many of the characters in *Hobson's Island* think that they are ideas that they have thought up for themselves. The book provides a list of characters, which is useful, as Themerson's characters are many and varied, and often bizarre and eccentric, although always individual, "real," and believable. Some, such as the Italian Princess Zuppa and her Polish friend Dr Goldfinger, have appeared in previous novels, but it isn't absolutely essential to have read about them before, and *Hobson* tells us quite enough about them for its own purposes. Here, the Princess and the Doctor have occasion to consult Cardinal Pölätüo, who, in 1962, had his own Themerson book in which they all appeared for the first time (though we had to wait another twenty odd years to be told something of their background.) The Cardinal is still living in his Roman palazzo and still giving viable advice—although he was born in 1822.

Personally, I am convinced that Stefan knew much more about his characters than he had time to tell us, and he probably liked to keep some of his knowledge back from book to book—maybe so as to surprise the reader. One of the characters of vital importance to the others, General Pięść, appears in *Hobson*'s list only as "absent," and this is because he is dead. His importance to the characters is that he fathered three of them—somewhat casually, it would seem—although we should *not* be particularly surprised, I think, that these three characters all existed before we ever heard of the gallant Polish

General, which was in 1976, when he too was given his own book: *General Pięść or the Forgotten Mission*.

The General's three offspring here in *Hobson* are Lady Cooper, Princess Zuppa, and the mysterious black ex-President of Bukumia. We have not heard of this "Dr Janson" before, and that makes us all the more curious: Is he really *not* a bastard—in the conversational sense of the word? Is he *really* a good guy who wanted to bring about a good revolution? We know just enough about Princess Zuppa for our needs, although no one ever seems to have told her who her mother was. We were told a good deal about the charming old Lady Cooper in the 1986 *Mystery of the Sardine*, and there we also heard the sad story of the General's fourth and last—post-humous—child, Ian Prentice, the mathematical genius who wrote his life's work, *Euclid Was an Ass*, and then died at the age of twelve.

In *The Chair of Decency*, Stefan told the Dutch academics, "It is a pity that the truth about original virtue, the virtue of bio-logical gentleness, has been engulfed in our lore by the cultural invention of original sin, the sin of natural evil." In *Hobson*, alas, the several sophisticated characters who represent their various countries' establishments and secret services demon-strate plenty of natural evil with their inhuman experiments, but surely, with the members of the Shepherd family, we are shown original virtue at its most attractive?

Stefan Themerson's novels are timeless. In the last two, in particular, he amused himself by acknowledging the slight influence of the detective stories he enjoyed reading by writers like Raymond Chandler. He was certainly good at suspense, and he also amused himself by producing some amazing coin-cidences. His basic plots were always so close to reality that he could afford to introduce—often in the most casual way—extremely fantastic occurrences. Towards the end of *Sardine*, we realize that the odd character called the Mad Hatter is in fact a man from Mars. But so what? And why not? The dramatic end of *Hobson* is also somewhat out of this world. But there has to be a first time for everything.

Barbara Wright
2005

# HOBSON'S
# ISLAND

# CONTENTS

## CAST OF CHARACTERS

THOMAS HOBSON

THOMAS GAMALIEL (T.G.H.) HOBSON 2 – *his son, fighter pilot from Alabama*

THOMAS LANCELOT (T.L.H.) HOBSON 3 – *son of T.G.H. and Prickly Rose*

MR AND MRS SHEPHERD

GREGORY SHEPHERD – *their son*

GEORGINA (GERALDINE) SHEPHERD – *their daughter*

LOUISE, JANE, PHILIP – *children of Georgina and Gregory*

J. K. WILKINSON SJ, *boatman* (*ex POW padre*)

CAPTAIN PAIN-IN-THE-NECK, *of* THE RESURRECTION

HERR SCHMIED, HERR FISCHER, HERR BRAUN *Swiss bankers* ('Les Amis de la Famille Shepherd')

DAVID D'EATH

SEAN D'EARTH (*sic*) – *his son*

PRICKLY ROSE – *Sean's wife*

ADAM D'EARTH – *their son*

LADY LUCY – *Adam's wife*

DEBORAH – *their daughter*

JOHN ST AUSTELL (Ostel) – *Deborah's friend* (*see also* 'The Chair of Decency' *and* 'The Mystery of the Sardine' *by the same author*)

A girl in the Cinéma-Cochon

GENERAL PIĘŚĆ – (*absent, see also* 'General Pięść')

LADY COOPER – *his daughter* (*see also* 'The Mystery of the Sardine')

PRINCESS ZUPPA – *his daughter* (*see also* 'General Pięść' *and* 'Cardinal Pölätüo')

PRESIDENT OF BUKUMLA – *his son*

AMALA – *President's mother*

MADAME B. – *Parisian bookseller*

HER NEPHEW – *who sells computers to Bukumla*

DR GOLDFINGER – *Zuppa's friend*

JONATHAN – *Cardinal Pölätüo's major-domo*

MAN IN THE ROOM WITH A PAINTED WINDOW – (*English secret service*)

PIERROT AND MARIE-CLAIRE – (*French secret service*)

NEMO

MATILDA – *the cow*

PART ONE

## ONE

## *The Weighing of the President*

When they (the French) rescued him, they didn't know who he was. Whatever they were doing there, prospecting, spying, hunting, or just walking about (who cares?), it was purely by coincidence that they found themselves in precisely that spot at precisely that moment. They were all armed. In that part of the world, one carried a gun as one carries a cheque book (&/or one of those plastic bank cards) in London, or a *carte d'identité* in Paris, or an engraved *carte de visite* in Warsaw.

'*Merde alors!*'

In front of them, behind the bushes, they saw six black men standing around another black man, his face of a different shade of blackness, ash-grey, perhaps with fear, some clotted blood above his eyebrow, his gold-capped teeth between his wide-open, thin, 'European' lips, chattering as he looked at the noose at the end of the rope hanging from a branch of the tree before him.

'*Haut les mains!*'

It doesn't matter in the least who fired the first shots, the pink French or the black Bukumlans. What matters is that it took the five Bukumlans two minutes to escape, and the sixth one another three minutes to die.

The smell of cordite spiced the smell of the jungle. They (the French) cut the rope with which the arms of the man with gold-capped teeth were tied behind his back.

'*Qui êtes-vous?*' they asked. '*Que se passe-t-il?*'

He didn't answer. Perhaps he couldn't, perhaps he didn't want to.

3

So they frisked him.

He was wearing a tailcoat, splashed with mud and a number of medals, and a boiled shirt crossed with the wide green ribbon of the Head of State.

*'Grands dieux! Monsieur le Président de Bukumla! Le salaud!'*

They didn't like it. They didn't want to be mixed up with local politics. They were in computers, which they called *'ordinateurs'*. Their business was to sell them, to introduce *l'ère de l'informatique* into the Third World. No, they didn't want to be involved. The present revolution in neighbouring Bukumla, well, no, *Il ne faut point se mêler dans leurs affaires*.

'What do you want us to do with you, Your Excellency?' they asked.

His Excellency didn't answer.

They gave him a sip of cognac from a hip flask. Then they knelt and examined the body of the dead man. In his pocket, they found an embossed card calling him 'The Honorary Treasurer of the Students' Union of the University of Bukumla'.

*'Ça alors! L'Association des Étudiants! Le Trésorier! Honorifique!'*

They laughed.

They thought they were tough (*dur à cuire*), and so they were. But they had just killed a man, and what for? To rescue that big bemedalled brute of a President? That wasn't funny.

So they laughed.

*'Le diable l'emporte!'*

They lifted the body of the Honorary Treasurer and hanged it by the neck from the noose swinging from the branch of the tree. Then they took one of His Excellency's orders and pinned it to the corpse. It was the papal order of the Holy Sepulchre. Red enamel cross potent, with small crosses between the arms. Had His Excellency ever been one of the noble pilgrims to Jerusalem? He must have, mustn't he? Unless he had bought it from Spinks. They couldn't leave his Excellency all alone with the corpse in the jungle, so they took him with them to their Station, a couple of miles away, at the sea coast, where

4

they sold him to a Mr Plain-Smith, the skipper of a boat which he referred to as a yacht, called, curiously, *The Resurrection*. It might have been that she was originally built for some missionaries but what she was carrying now was various kinds of ammunition.

Even generals tend to forget that once the ammunition is frittered away, the most sophisticated rifle isn't worth more than a length of iron water pipe. Mr Plain-Smith, who supplied his wares to the Republic of Bukumla regularly, knew His Excellency well and recognized him at once. But His Excellency didn't react. Didn't react at all. Had those bumps on his head made him a proper zombie or was he pretending to be one? They didn't know. And didn't care. It didn't matter. It was of no importance, considering . . . Considering what? Spinoza? *Sub specie aeternitatis?* Whenever he quoted Spinoza (or Wittgenstein), Mr Plain-Smith used to call himself Captain Plain-Smith, PhD, or just Dr Plain-Smith. By his crew, he liked to be called P.S.

'How much do you want for him?' he asked.

'*Eh bien*,' they said, '*Le Président de la République de Bukumla! Valoir son pesant d'or!*'

'His weight in gold? Shit!' he said. 'I'll give you his weight in whisky.'

'*Topez là!*'

'Shake!'

They (the French) had an electronic weighing machine. They stood His Excellency on it. And were disappointed. The President's weight was a mere 53.5 kilograms, hook, line and sinker; shoes, tails and medals. They fed their *ordinateur* with the relevant data:

* 1 litre of water weighs 1 kilogram;
* Absolute alcohol specific gravity is 0.789, meaning:
  1 litre of alcohol weighs 789 grams;
* 1 litre of whisky = 60% (volume) of water = 600 grams,

5

and 40% (ditto) of alcohol = 315 grams, which makes the weight of 1 litre of whisky = 915 grams;
* As a bottle of whisky contains ¾ litre, its weight = 686 grams;
* Now, the weight of His Excellency the President is 53.5 kilograms or 53,500 grams, which, divided by 686 grams per bottle, gives: 78 bottles.

Seventy-eight bottles of whisky were transferred from *The Resurrection* to the Station, upon which the dethroned President of the Republic of Bukumla was transferred from the Station to *The Resurrection*.

'*Bon débarras!*' they said, and opened a bottle of champagne.

•

'Good morning, sir. Your breakfast, sir. I've put the breakfast tray by your berth, sir. If you turn your head to the right, you'll see it, sir.'

Silence.

And then the voice from the berth said: 'Who are you?'

'I'm your steward, sir. Enjoy your breakfast, sir.'

The door clicked shut.

He called himself 'steward', and he said the 'berth', so this must be a boat, and this up-and-down and to-and-fro feeling must be the sea . . . the waves . . . the . . . he turned his head to the right, as he had been told to do, and he opened his eyes, only just. Through his eyelashes he saw the breakfast tray: a glass of orange juice, cereal, ham and eggs on a hot metal dish, toast, marmalade, coffee . . . He closed his eyes and repeated: *orange juice, cereal, ham and eggs, toast, marmalade, coffee* . . . and then the void returned, the long void, the long nothingness, till the voice sounded again:

'Good morning, sir. Your breakfast, sir. Nice weather, sir. The sea has calmed down, sir. Enjoy your breakfast, sir.'

## The Weighing of the President

Click.

He opened his eyes. He was wearing pyjamas he had never seen before. He looked up. There was a little round window through which he saw the blue sky. He turned his head to the right. There was his breakfast tray . . . orange juice, cereal, kippers, toast, marmalade, coffee . . . He closed his eyes and repeated: *orange juice, cereal, kippers . . . Kippers?* So this is not the same breakfast . . . So this is not the same morning . . . So it must be Friday . . . His old mother, Amala, eats fish on Fridays. The General got her into the habit of eating fish on Fridays. The General. His father, the General. His white father, the General. His Polish white father, the General. He had never seen his father. Except in the photograph. On a white horse. When the General suddenly appeared there, during the Second World War, before Bukumla became Bukumla, suddenly, suddenly out of the blue he had appeared from nowhere, appeared from nowhere and made love to the beautiful young black girl Amala Amalamala Alamalama, who a year later gave birth to a little black boy, upon which he, the General, disappeared, suddenly, disappeared, as Amala said, for patriotic reasons, disappeared for patriotic reasons from what is now the Republic of Bukumla and appeared for patriotic reasons in the Republic of Italy where he made love to a young Italian married lady who a year later gave birth to Princess Zuppa, his, the present President's, half-sister, upon which he, the General, her father, disappeared again, for patriotic reasons, to appear, for patriotic reasons, in England. Or did he appear in Italy before appearing in Bukumla? Was Princess Zuppa a year older than he, her half-brother, or a year younger? He couldn't be sure now. The beautiful Princess Zuppa. Completely white. *Completamente, interamente* white. As white as the White Horse of the General. He, the present President of Bukumla, well . . . is he still the present President? All right then, he, the dethroned President, whom they are going to hang, unless they have already done so? Have

7

they already hanged him? Is he already dead? He should have opened his eyes when that Voice said: 'I am your steward, sir', he should have had looked whether the Voice had wings, white wings, wings . . . all God's children had white wings . . . '*White wings*' he repeated, and then the void returned, the long void, the long nothingness, till the Voice sounded again:

'Good morning, sir. Your breakfast, sir. And this time you must eat it, sir. Captain's orders.'

He opened his eyes and looked at the steward. The steward had no wings. He was a young man, tall, slim, blue-eyed, blond, pink-faced, and good-humouredly smiling. Then he looked at the breakfast tray. Orange juice, cereal, ham and eggs . . . No more fish. Ham. So this must be Saturday.

'Come on, sir. Start eating. You haven't touched any food for three days, sir. The Captain said I wasn't to leave you until you'd finished your breakfast.'

'I'll have some coffee,' he said.

He drank coffee, then he ate some toast with marmalade, then the ham and eggs, then the cereal, and topped it all with the glass of orange juice.

'Nicely done, sir,' the steward said. 'But sort of back to front.'

'Back to life,' His Excellency said.

'That suits us, sir. As our name is *The Resurrection*.'

•

'. . . good luck to you, sir.' The Captain lifted his glass of brandy.

'I don't know why, and perhaps I shouldn't, but I trust you, Skipper.'

'You can trust me so long as you are not under the illusion that I may disobey the orders I get from my masters.'

'Perhaps I wouldn't if I thought you might.' He took a puff

8

at his cigar. 'I wish I had spoken to you when I saw you at my Ministry of Defence . . .' He mused upon what he had just said. 'You see, you know all about me, I know so little about you . . .'

'All right, my dear fellow,' Mr Plain-Smith, the Captain, said. 'I'm going to tell you about myself, for your instruction and for my pleasure. Reminiscences make me feel philosophical, and so I'm going to tell you how at the time of the London blitz I was evacuated with other kids to a place in the country which happened to be the mansion of an admiral, where I fell in love both with the sea and a female literary agent five times my age whose deity was Schopenhauer, which fact, some years later – for inscrutable are the workings of Providence – made me read Spinoza: *De Intellectus Emendatione*, meaning "How to improve your mind", and *Tractatus Politicus*, in which he tells you how he had tried not to laugh at human actions, not to weep at them, nor to hate them, but to understand them. Now, what's that?' he pressed some buttons on the intercom:

. . . SEVERE GALE FORCE 9 IMMINENT

The Captain got up.

'I'm going to be busy now, my dear fellow. Please go to your cabin, and I'll see you later.'

He put two cigars into the breast pocket of the ex-President's white tunic, a box of matches into his side pocket, and handed him the bottle with what remained of the brandy in it. When they were at the door, he asked:

'Want anything to read?'

'No, thank you.'

And then he changed his mind.

'Yes, can you give me the Bible, if you have one? I mean, if you have one to spare.'

•

It was unfortunate that the fatal wireless weather forecast was reported to Mr Plain-Smith, the Captain, just at the time when he felt himself warming towards the President, for this conference, meeting, interview (whatever it is right to call it) started in a much more formal and not especially very friendly manner.

When His Excellency, the President, was 'summoned' to the Captain's cabin, he refused to go there in his pyjamas, which – by the way – were not actually his. They provided him with his own black trousers, but – judging that his boiled shirt and bemedalled tails were not suitable for the occasion (though cleaned and ironed by the boat's laundryman) – they gave him a T-shirt (belonging to one of the crew) and a white (officer's) tunic.

The Captain's cabin (unless you prefer to call it a stateroom) looked more like an intellectual don's study. There were books on the shelves, protected by a metal grid against the wobbly arrow of gravity, pictures screwed to the wall, a big desk littered with papers secured by some heavy objects, paperweights, stones, a magazine of cartridges.

'Sit yourself down, Your Excellency,' the Captain said. 'You look much better, sir. I hope you are fully restored from your recent setback.'

'What I wish to know . . .' the President started, but Mr Plain-Smith was too quick for him.

'Yes, of course,' he said. 'We'll come to that in a moment. Incidentally, we have already met on one or two occasions, if you recall . . .'

'Could you refresh my memory?'

'I used to supply some goods to your Ministry of Defence, sir.'

'Ironmongery?'

'Not exactly. The Russians were giving you plenty of hardware but only a token amount of ammunition. We were selling you ammunition that fitted the Russian guns to make you less dependent on them.'

'Very ingenious, Captain. So we are old acquaintances. And perhaps you'll be good enough to tell me where I am, what I am doing here, how I have . . .'

'In a moment, sir. But first . . . a drink? A cigarette? A cigar.'

'Perhaps a little later . . .'

'Well, sir, you know there was a revolution in Bukumla . . .'

'Yes, I do.'

'And I suppose you remember . . . well, what is the last thing you do remember?'

'The last thing I remember is that I was going to be hanged. I must confess that at some moments I'm not sure that I haven't . . .'

'No, you haven't, sir. You've been rescued, sir.'

'By you?'

'I don't claim that honour. You were rescued by some French computer missionaries. My privilege is that of giving you the hospitality of *The Resurrection*.'

'Thank you. Will you tell me how I can give my thanks also to my rescuers?'

'That is neither possible nor advisable.'

'Yes?'

'It is not possible because they are not here. It is not advisable because it would embarrass them.'

'Yes?'

'You see, they killed a man.'

'Yyess?'

'I called them computer missionaries. Actually, they are computer salesmen. But they behaved like students, which they were years ago. In 1968, in Paris.'

'Yes?'

'You see, they killed a man. And they panicked. And when they panicked, they did something silly. They hanged the dead body from the noose that had been prepared for you and pinned one of your medals to it.'

'How gruesome.'

11

'It wasn't meant to be gruesome. It was meant to prove their machismo.'

'I see.'

'But that's not all, sir. When I went to that place in the jungle the next morning to see the body, it wasn't there. Vanished.'

'Termites?'

'No, the termites couldn't possibly have digested the enamel of your papal order of the Holy Sepulchre. And the order wasn't there. Obviously, the corpse was snatched. Either by your enemies, to have evidence of the historical truth of your death, or by your friends, to build an underground shrine where they would celebrate the historical truth of your martyrdom.'

'Why do you say "the historical truth of my death", Captain? The historical truth is that I am alive.'

'Well, sir. Not really. Your being alive is the physical truth. Your being dead is the historical truth. You see, sir, physical truths are caused by some events that took place in the past. Like the fact that the present position of a billiard ball depends on the way it was pushed in the past. It is just the opposite with historical truths. Historical truths are caused by some events in the future. Like the truth about miracles. The reality of miracles does not depend on the chemical analysis of Bread, Wine and Blood. Nor does it depend on some historical facts of the past. It is future beliefs that cause their historical truth.'

'You mean, Captain, that future beliefs will make the dead corpse *be me*?'

'Precisely. That's to say, if we don't do anything about it.'

'We? Meaning you and me?'

'Meaning you and my masters. Meaning also the future Bukumla exiles whom you can lead.'

The President looked at the tips of the fingers of his closed left hand and moved them slightly, one after another, as if he were counting them. Then he said: 'My gold-capped teeth

12

must be as indigestible for the termites as the papal order is, and so their absence may become more significant than the order's presence.'

'It's unlikely that they would perform an autopsy now, whoever they are. We, yes, we could do it sometime in the future. If we find it necessary. And if we find the hanged man's body.'

'Yes, the body . . .' the President said. 'Who was it? Do you know?'

'I don't know his name. The French boy said he was *Le Trésorier* of the Students' Union of the University of Bukumla.'

'Oh dear, dear me. I'm sorry,' the President said.

'Did you say you were sorry, sir?'

'Yes. Shouldn't I be?'

'The man was going to murder you, sir.'

'Yes. I know. Should it make a difference?'

'A very Christian attitude of mind . . .' the Captain said, without a wince.

'I'm not a Christian in the religious sense of the term.'

'Is there any other sense in which one can be a Christian?'

'Yes, of course, Captain. Most of you, Europeans, are Christians in a non-religious sense. Including your Jews and your atheists.'

The sun lights, reflected from the green waves beyond, struck upwards through the porthole and quivered and gleamed on the low ceiling of the cabin.

'With all due respect, Mr President, sir, I must confess how deeply puzzled I find myself. Please, don't take umbrage at what I'm going to ask. But . . . you yourself know that you could hardly be described as a . . . liberal ruler. You ruled the country with an iron fist. It was not without reason that people called you a ruthless, bloodthirsty tyrant. Now, sir, how is it that you don't give that sort of impression to me now?'

The sky beyond must have clouded over as the lights on the ceiling stopped dancing and vanished.

'You were offering me a cigar, Captain. I would accept it now.'

'Yes, of course,' Mr Plain-Smith opened the box. 'And brandy?' he asked and reached for the bottle. 'Well then,' he started again, somewhat diffidently, 'speaking as man to man . . . ?'

'All right,' the President said, 'man to man. Or, better still, skipper to skipper. Think for a moment that you are in command of a strange kind of ship. She is so big that from your top-mast you can't see where the hell her beams are. And she isn't on course in any direction in space. She just bubbles up through time. And the day you take command of her, you discover that each bubble is bursting with the gas of hatred and corruption and greed and the worst kind of lies. Because there are three kinds of lying. Lying to others is just an ordinary sort of thing, we all do it, sometimes for the sake of the people we are lying to, not for our own. Then there is lying to oneself. Which isn't too bad so long as you know that you are fundamentally all right. But then there are those who lie to themselves and believe their own lies. They are the worst kind. Because they are prepared to kill themselves and to kill you for the sake of their lies. Now, Skipper, what would you do if you had to lead such a crew? Would you start by setting up a parliamentary democracy? Electioneering? Voting? A Referendum? *Vox populi*? Worship the Sacred Cow of the Majority? All the time knowing that any 51 per cent will vote for making the remaining 49 walk the plank? Blindfolded.'

'I see that you had your problems,' the Captain admitted.

'Indeed, I had my problems. My main problem was that the time was not ripe. My problem was my knowledge that people are capable of doing anything. That a parliamentary majority is capable of doing any bloody thing. Therefore some things must be excluded from its competence. They must be excluded before the system is set up. Excluded from the Majority's competence must be precisely those primary things that must

14

be accepted as self-evident. And if the Majority doesn't accept them as self-evident, then they must be imposed from the Outside. Preferably by a God. But if His commandments are unworkable, or silly, or sissy, as the case may be, then they have to be imposed by human force, which task is neither easy nor pleasant.'

'Do you mean things like "love one another"?'

'My dear Skipper, you know perfectly well that is not what I mean. You can't force people to love one another. You can't force them even to like being loved. It would be more practical to tell them "you shall not hate one another", but that, too, constricts the liberty of their feelings. Though, yes, the form of such a command is more reasonable. Because futile and enslaving are commandments in the form of "*do!*". If you want people to be free, the commandments must be in the form *"don't!"* Like *"Défense d'uriner"*, which obliges you, the ruler, to provide them with *pissoirs*. Or like "You shall not kill", which obliges you to provide them with a state of peace. Or like "You shall not steal", which obliges you to provide them with some other means of satisfying their hunger and their greed. Or like *"neminem captivabimus nisi iure victum"*, which obliges you to provide them with uncorrupted justice. Well, that's it, Skipper.'

'No, it isn't,' the Captain said. 'You forget that you yourself didn't obey your own commandments.'

'Neither did God, did He? God, too, didn't obey His own commandments. He wasn't naïve enough to be like a nice primary-school schoolteacher who's supposed to set a good example to children.'

'His Son was,' the Captain said.

'Yes. And got Himself tortured and crucified. Is that a good example to set to children? Hasn't He glorified the very existence of torture and death in the Arsenal of the means that are supposed to be justified by the ends?'

'Don't get me wrong, my dear fellow,' the Captain said

quickly. 'I, too, have supplied some "means" to the Arsenal of your Ministry of Defence, and I'm not a preacher. I told you what puzzled me. I summon you here, and what do I see? I see a wise, warmhearted man who tells me he's sorry for a chap who intended to murder him. On the other hand, what I knew about you was that you were a ruthless autocrat, committing all kinds of evil brutalities.'

'I *was* committing all kinds of evil brutalities.'

'Knowing that evil creates evil and sooner or later people will respond with their own kind of evil brutalities?'

'Knowing that they will respond with revolution.'

'Which will topple you!'

'Yes. And show that the time is ripe. Yes,' he repeated in a dry and level tone of voice. 'And do get it into your head, please, that I'm *not* on the side of my praetorian guard. I'm on the side of that poor boy, the *Trésorier* of the Students' Union. And if your masters in London think that they can make me call on Bukumlan nationalists and new exiles to unite and create what they think of as a free democratic nation, well . . . then you'd better stop the boat and let me go.'

'Where would you like to go?'

'You know very well where to. Where we all, kings, presidents, dictators, stow our lifebelts away in numbered bank accounts: Switzerland, Liechtenstein, Luxemburg . . .'

'Three countries with no access to the sea . . .'

'Quite,' he said. And then asked, pleasantly, 'Now, Skipper, how much can you tell me? Can you tell me where we are going?'

'Our present course is nor-norwest.'

'And our destination? Or should I have said "destiny"?'

'I think they want to put you on ice.'

'In a morgue?'

'No. In some nice safe place. Till they make up their minds how to use you later, if necessary. Look, my dear fellow, you don't need to worry. My present orders are exactly what you'd like them to be. First: to keep mum about you. Second: to give you a new name.'

'Can you do that?'

'Of course I can. I'm the Captain. I've the right to issue birth certificates.'

'To newborn babies?'

'Well, you're being re-born. What's the difference? *Hic mortuus est* the President of the Republic of Bukumla, *hic natus est* . . . well, what sort of name should I give you? Any name, except Smith, please.'

They regarded each other steadily for a whole minute. Then the President said: 'My father's Christian name was Jan. Spelled J-A-N. I want to be called Janson.'

'Excellent, Mr Janson,' the Captain said.

'You may as well call me Dr Janson. I have some half a dozen doctorates *honoris causa*.'

'You still need a Christian name, Dr Janson. Nothing timid. It must be something very bold.'

'Archibald?'

The Captain lifted his glass of brandy: ' . . . *hic natus est* Dr Archibald Janson! Good luck to you, sir.'

•

She was sitting at a large desk, her back to the window. Looking from the street at this tower block, only some very high officials (and perhaps some spies) would know which window it was.

Ages ago, before the time of the computer, when she worked in Decoding by turning the mysterious analytical wheels of enciphered probability with her own hands, she was a full-of-life, bright and pretty young lady, a daughter of one-of-those-families whose loyalty did not need to be investigated. Today, her daughter (who didn't care a damn for any coding or decoding) was a full-of-life and pretty, and very slim

17

young Ms, while she herself seemed to have grown laterally, her bones had thickened, and the bulk of her body settled itself firmly in her swivel chair.

She was looking at two A4 sheets of paper on her desk, one on her left, the other on her right, and she smiled. Not at their content. She had stopped bothering about the contents of any communication long ago. She smiled at their style. So different. The piece on the left was from the Consul (the Honorary Consul in Bukumla, there was neither an Embassy nor a proper Consulate in Bukumla), and it read as if it had been written a hundred years ago. The one on the right, perversely, might have been written by a schoolboy playing a noble pirate, and it came from the captain of *The Resurrection*, Mr Plain-Smith, whom they used to call here 'Pain-Smith', or just 'Pain-in-the-neck'.

The epistle on the left read as follows:

. . . It has become my distressing duty to announce to you that last night his Excellency, the President of the Republic of Bukumla, was abducted, about the hour of half-past 10, from his private box at Kennedy's Theatre, in the city. The President about 8 o'clock accompanied Madame Amala, his Mother, to the theatre. Another lady and gentleman were with them in the box. About half-past 10, during a pause in the performance, five or six men entered the box, the door of which was unguarded, hastily approached the President from behind, put a pistol to the back of his head, and marched him out. One of the men then leaped from the box upon the stage brandishing a large knife or dagger, and exclaiming '*Sic semper tyrannis!*' (which are, as I recollect, the very words uttered by the assassin of President Lincoln some hundred and twenty years ago), and escaped in the rear of the theatre.

I am constantly receiving reports which lead to show that the President was taken into the jungle where he was assassinated by his abductors; that the bodyguard, so unpardonably absent in the theatre, caught up with the abductors, killed them, and buried the body of the President some place at the very border of Bukumla; that the insurgents caught up with the bodyguard, murdered them all, and obliterated the grave; and that horrible as are the atrocities that have been resorted to by the insurgents, they are not likely in any degree to impair the public spirit or postpone the complete and final overthrow of the rebellion; but similar reports have so often proved false, that for my own part I feel unable to indulge in any forecast of probabilities.

In profound grief for the events which it has become my duty to communicate to you, I have the honour to be

very respectfully,

Your obedient servant,

*E. M. Stanton Jnr.*

Hon. Con.

The paper on her right, a transcript of the radio message, read as follows:

Bloody whole gale too much for *The Resurrection*. Blown off course. Helluva way west. Which makes no difference as you don't bother to tell where and when you want me to be.

The passenger is all right. I baptized him yesterday. He's now Dr Archibald Janson. Sounds OK. Nice fellow. But I must warn you:

1.  Don't take it for granted he'll be on the side of his followers. He might well join the rebels who have dethroned him.
2.  He's more European than you, me, and all of us British. You must treat him accordingly. As you would . . . let me think . . . well . . . let's say Prince Rainier of Monaco

or – why not? – Le Suzerain of Andorra, The Rt. Revd the Bishop of Urgel.

3. Remember: all he's got on him (apart from a T-shirt & the officer's tunic we gave him) is: a pair of dirty socks, *ditto* underpants, a boiled shirt, tails, and all his medals, except the papal order of the Holy Sepulchre which, as I told you in my very first message, the French took to decorate the macabre Christmas Tree of their own making. My steward will send you Dr Janson's measurements.

4. Incidentally: he hasn't got a fucking farthing on him. In Bukumla, the President doesn't need to carry any money. Which doesn't mean that sometime in the future he'll be not able to repay you &c. &c.

5. And don't forget a toothbrush and books, 'library books'. French and English.

Now, can't you decide something? Don't make me wait around in the open sea. Personally, I don't care a damn where I am, but he's a decent fellow, I don't want him to think he's a Prisoner on *The Resurrection*.

Give this hum of mine to a pro to put it in a proper lingo before it goes higher up.

Love and x x x
Yrs *Pain-in-the-neck*


She got up. She walked round her desk, picked up the top edge of the radio message between the thumb and forefinger of her left hand, the Consul's report with those of her right hand, and holding them in the air, turned towards *the* door. The door had no knob and no keyhole. She pushed it with her knee and went in.

The only window in the room was the one painted on the blind wall. It was a beautiful *trompe-l'oeil* window and it cheered up the room though you couldn't open it, you couldn't jump out of it, you couldn't change the colour of the sky which was blue and sunny even when it was raining and even in the middle of the night.

On the wall opposite the painted window was a painted door. The painted door had a beautiful *trompe-l'oeil* doorhandle and a keyhole, and it was slightly ajar, just enough to notice a painted shadow lurking behind it.

Between the painted window on one wall and the painted door on another, stood a real, three-dimensional desk. She walked to it and, without saying a word, put the two A4 sheets of paper on it. The man behind the desk raised his grey, bushy eyebrows. She nodded. He must have been trained in fast reading. It took him seconds to go through both papers.

'Well, what do you think?' he asked.

'I stopped thinking a long time ago,' she answered.

' "*Dr Archibald Janson*",' he quoted.

'Well, why not?' she said. 'As good a name as any other.'

'Could he be an impostor?' he asked.

'Definitely not,' she said. 'Why?'

'The Consul says the real President was assassinated.'

'The Consul pens his letter with a quill feather. Sounds quite refreshing. But what he says is all hearsay. What the Captain says is facts. And he had met the President before all that started. He couldn't make a mistake.'

'Couldn't he act in collusion?'

'Our Pain-in-the-neck? Definitely not.'

'So we take *his* report as a working hypothesis?'

'We take it as the gospel truth,' she said.

He took the paper on his left and put it aside.

'Well?' she asked.

'Well what?'

'Well, what do we do? We can't keep them in their *Resurrection* bobbing up and down in the middle of the ocean till the Last Day.'

'I suppose not,' he said.

'Nothing from the Cabinet Office?' she asked.

'Nothing.'

'That's strange, isn't it? They were all so excited about it at the beginning.'

'Well, yes, but that's because they didn't know.'

'What did they not know?'

'They didn't know where Bukumla was.'

'How do you mean, they didn't?'

'Well, you see, they mixed it with Bugulma.'

'What?'

'Bugulma.'

'Bugulma?!'

'Bugulma.'

'God Almighty!' she exclaimed. 'You don't mean that place in Soviet Russia?'

'I do. 54 33 N 52 40 E. Industrial town in Tatar Republic. Or rather the Tatar autonomous region of the Soviet Union.'

'And they thought it was there that the rebellion started! No wonder they were so excited.'

'Quite. And when I told them it wasn't Bugulma but Bukumla, and Bukumla happens to be in Africa, they blamed me. As if it was I who started the revolution in the wrong place.' He looked at her with a twinkle in his eye, and said, 'Now they think it is the French, and I don't dare tell them that the only French we know there are a few students and computer salesmen scared stiff by what has happened. So they, in the Cabinet Office, insist it must be the French, but they aren't sure: Was it in a French-backed coup that the President was overthrown? – in which case we should be on his side, or: Was he supported by the French? – in which case we should be on the side of the rebels. They can't make up their minds so they're waiting.'

'For what?'

'For the Americans.'

22

'Can't they decide anything without asking the Americans?'

'No, it isn't that,' he said. 'They're waiting for the Americans to burn their fingers first.'

For a brief moment, they looked at each other in silence. Years of co-operation had tuned them in to each other so that it now looked as if they could read each other's thoughts. 'Well?' he said drily, and she knew that he had already made a decision, and she knew what it was.

'Hobson's Island?' she asked.

'Yes, Hobson's Island. There's no other choice. We can't have him here till we see which way Downing Street jumps.'

He looked at the painted window and his eyes were focused miles away, as if he could see through it. Then he bent over his desk, put his forefinger on the Captain's report, and said: 'Dear Lucy, we shall do exactly as our Pain-in-the-neck tells us. The steward will wire you Dr Janson's measurements. You'll go to Savile Row and buy him some suits, you'll go to Jermyn Street and buy him some shirts and underpants, you'll go to Fortnum and Mason and buy him some toiletry, you'll go to Hatchards and buy him some books English and French, and you'll go to Marks and Spencer and buy a few yards of red carpet. Then you'll take a helicopter to Hobson's Island and organize the reception of His Excellency the ex-President of Bukumla.' He reflected for a moment, and then added, 'You can take your daughter with you.'

'Deborah? I wonder . . .' she said

'Why?' he asked, without looking at her. For a fraction of a second he glanced at the painted door, but then his eyes started to observe the top of his desk again. 'Lucy,' he said, 'your daughter wouldn't leak anything to the press?'

'No, nothing of that sort,' she said. 'It's only . . . It's just her new phase. She's now a hyper-super-post-punk. She shaves strange bald patches on her head, she hangs atrocious jewellery from her ears, she wears a wide white trouser on her left leg and a narrow black one on her right, she paints her fingernails all in different colours, she is a pretty girl and she does everything to look incredibly ugly. There's a sort of philosophical arrogance in it. You see, she wants to be loved *not* for her looks. And she has the impudence to think that she can afford that sort of thing. And it seems that she can.'

'My dear Lucy,' he said. 'All this sounds so charmingly innocent.'

'I suppose it does,' she said. 'I suppose it is. But if she appears so made-up in front of the President of Bukumla, he's bound to suspect that she's making fun of him by imitating some African tribal custom.'

'No. Not if he is more European than Prince Rainier of Monaco or the Bishop of Urgel.'

'I'm afraid that's not all there is to it. I'm afraid she has a peculiar talent for provoking people . . .'

'Sex?' he asked.

'No,' she said. 'Poetry. She writes what her friends call "poetry", and she thinks it's her mission to read it aloud and impose it on people. And it's a curious kind of poetry. A mixture of what seems to be ultra-modern, anti-art, aleatory, whatever that means, disjointed *vers libre*, with orthodox nineteenth-century Tennysonian metric stanzas. But she does it in such an obscene, perverse way, you see, it's in her avant-garde, jumpy free verse that she uses such words as rosy-fingered dawn, and the iron tongue of midnight, and air-built castles, and sea-girt isle, and blissful morn and eve and thou and ye, and breezy blue, and of course the daffodils and balms and palms and alms . . . And it is in her regular metric old-fashioned stanzas that she says fuck, and shit, and prick, and cunt, and all those monosyllabic nouns – God Almighty knows what they are really meant to mean.'

His eyes still fixed on the top of his desk, he asked: 'Drugs?'

'Fortunately, not. Well, not really.'

Now he lifted his head and looked at her, and he looked as if he were gazing at himself in the mirror.

'Lucy,' he said. 'You don't know how lucky you are.'

## TWO

## D'Eath into D'Earth

Her (Deborah's) father's father was born in a little thatched cottage (half in Sussex half in Surrey) on the 31st December of 1899 and baptized (by his own father) a week later, which means that his flesh belonged to the nineteenth century while his soul was awakened to the twentieth. It means also that he was too young to take part in the First World War which ended in 1918, and too old for active service in the Second World War which started towards the end of 1939.

As he was preparing to join the Army in 1918 (which he never did because the War ended in that year) one of the things that worried not only him but also some superstitious civil servants who kept putting his papers at the bottom of the pile, was his name. His surname. Most embarrassing. Especially for a soldier. He was called Sean D'Eath. They said: He couldn't possibly join the Army with such a name. Thus, he decided to change it. By deed poll. His father (Deborah's father's father's father) didn't like the idea. By profession, he was many things, all at the same time: teacher of the ignorant on the flute, cornopean, first fiddle, horn, and bugle (the second fiddle was played by the shoemaker, the bassoon by the baker, and clarinet by the butcher), he was also: brewer of small beer, Parish Clerk and half Curate, Collector of Taxes, Land measurer, Assistant Overseer, Postmaster, and Collector of debts. 'Son,' he said, 'keep this in mind. In your entry of baptism the word "*gent.*" is inserted after my name (he forgot that it was he himself who had written the entry), as our name is a very honourable name. There is – in Belgium – a place called Ath. And, do you remember? – no, of course not, it was just before you were born – men putting up posts and rails on The Hill to the right of The Lane, in digging struck something hard, which proved to be a skull. The skull was a most marked example of Belgic type. Couldn't that have been the skull of our ancestor who came *De* the place called *Ath*?'

But Rose, the daughter of the stockbroker who was commuting (even in wartime) between the village and the Stock Exchange, London, the beautiful though prickly English rose, told him: 'My dear Mr D'Eath, your name is a camouflaged "death" which once upon a time was a nickname for one who played the part of Death in pageants and plays.' He blushed. She was some two years older, she was busy writing the History of the Village, she looked at him with an air of authority. 'Unless . . .' she added, 'unless D'Eath is the first syllable of Deathridge or Deathwright, which some six hundred years ago meant "Executioner" or "Murderer".'

He knew, of course, that all that etymological nonsense would count for nothing in the trenches. Here comes Private First Class D'Eath! Oh God! Go away! *Nomen omen!* We don't want you! Well, so that's that. He must change his name. 'If you must, you must,' his father said, 'but try to keep the *D* and apostrophe, or *De*, it gives the name a noble air of panache which you deserve.'

And so they tried: Sean De Life, and Sean D'Elife; Sean De Light, and Sean D'Elight; and De la Vie, and D'Eflower, and D'Elouse, and D'Emigod, and D'Emijohn, and D'Emimonde.

They had great fun, father and son, inventing new names,
Sean D'Uster, the father said, Sean D'Aft, the son said,
they drank their small beer and laughed,
Sean D'Esire, the son said, Sean D'Ysuria, the father said;
Sean D'Ildo, the son said, Sean D'Ammit the father reprimanded . . . . ,
they had a good time, but when they arrived at Sean D'Entifrice, it sobered them up.

'What about Sean D'Earth?' Sean said.

'Sounds good,' his father said. 'Makes me think of John Lackland.'

Thus Sean D'Eath became Sean D'Earth, but in the meantime Kaiser Wilhelm fled to Holland, the war was won without Sean's help, whereupon he joined the local Tory party, became its councillor, married the Prickly Rose and, following her father's profession, became a stockbroker.

•

He had been a stockbroker for forty-three years, till he retired at the age of sixty-three and forgot all about it. If one startled him with, 'You used to be a stockbroker, usen't you?' he would ask, 'What?' and it would take a long while till his mind turned 180 degrees from the present and allowed him to say, 'Oh yes, that's right,' upon which it would quickly go the further 180 degrees, back to the present.

In the year he retired, in the middle of the sixties, he stopped reading the *Financial Times* and the *Wall Street Journal*, ten years later he stopped reading *The Times* and the *Daily Telegraph*, and ten years later still, he stopped reading the *Guardian*. During all those twenty or so years of his retirement, it was once, and only once, that he did something connected with that financial world within which he had lived for more than forty years, and that was only because of her. Lady Cooper. He hadn't seen her, or heard from her, for a long time when suddenly she telephoned him asking whether he could do something useful for a foreign mission from Bukumla, Africa, concerned with Technical and Investment Development. He didn't know why she was so interested in Bukumla, of all places, and he didn't ask. He never could say *No* to her. And so he said he would. And he did. He put them in touch with an American Pole, resident in London, who knew everything about the financial, industrial and biotechnical business of introducing battery-hen batteries into the tropical climate parts

28

of the world. A pioneering job. Not unlike Henri IV's *'I want there to be no peasant in my kingdom so poor that he is unable to have a chicken in his pot every Sunday.'*

The chicken didn't save the king. Henri IV was assassinated by a fanatic, Ravaillac by name. Which was bad for Europe. The subsequent quartering of the regicide's body didn't improve things. Wouldn't it be just the opposite in Bukumla? Wouldn't some nice killing of the President of Bukumla be good for Africa? Now, will not those battery hens save him from being done away with? Why should he, Sean D'Earth, yes . . . why must he think about it, it is not his business to know whether it is more important to feed people than to get rid of a bully. He, Sean D'Earth, had retired, hadn't he? He had left all that kind of speculation behind him. Why should he, Sean D'Earth, interfere now with some other people's history just because she, Lady Cooper, asked him to do something for them?

•

He first met her towards the end of the war. The Second World War. In the First World War young men were sent to the trenches indiscriminately. In the Second, scientists were sent to laboratories, writers to the BBC, painters to camouflage the roofs of factories, and stockbrokers to the Ministry of Supply. That's where he met Lady Cooper, who looked so smart in her WRAC uniform. It was before she married Sir Lionel and became Lady Cooper. It might have been – who can tell? – that she would have become not a Lady Cooper but a Mrs D'Earth had it not been for Prickly Rose who, at the age of just over forty, bore him a son and became more and more prickly. It was a Caesarean section performed to the accompaniment of the shrieking air-raid sirens and the burst of a bomb. She said it was all his fault, even the bomb. He said he was sorry and went down to the Naafi cafeteria where, when he asked for a cup of tea, the girl looked at him and said: 'You just sit down, I'll bring it to you.' When she did, she saw two tears running down his face, and – as it was after the air raid – she asked, 'What is it, duckie?'

'My wife has just given birth to a child,' he said.

'So you should be jumping for joy,' she said.

'I am,' he said.

And then a lady officer who was sitting at his table, beside him, asked: 'Is it a boy or a girl?'

He looked at her. 'A boy,' he said.

She lifted her cup of tea, and said: 'This is to your son, *prosit!*'

And he said 'Thank you,' and he was overwhelmed by the fact that the Blitz was making everybody so warm and friendly, and –

'What will you call him?' the lady officer asked.

'Adam,' he said without thinking, 'Adam D'Earth.'

'Oh,' she said, 'that's the name of our great bard, Adam Mickiewicz.'

'I beg your pardon?' he said.

'Well, I was born in Poland,' she said, and the same evening they went to a little cinema not far from Paddington Station to see *Gone with the Wind*.

•

He never (well, hardly ever) thought of leaving his Prickly Rose (after all, it was she who left him at the end). His little son was the centre of his affections now. He wouldn't be separated from him. He, Sean D'Earth, might not need a wife, but he knew that his son Adam needed a mother. Of that, he was dead certain. When he himself was a small boy . . . his own mother . . . oh, well, that was the time when women, who paid taxes, were stone-throwing, window-smashing, to make the government realize that they were entitled to the

30

protection and privilege of the vote on the same terms as men who paid taxes. No, his mother had nothing to do with what *The Times* used to call the 'Outrages by Suffragists'. But, as always, it is the bystanders, with whom the learned historians do not identify themselves, it is the anonymous onlookers who pay the price for their saviours' idealisms. What his mother was doing there, in London, at that particular time and place, he didn't know. Perhaps she had gone there to see a friend? Perhaps she had gone there to buy something she couldn't buy in the village? Anyway, what happened was that when a placard bearing the words VOTES FOR WOMEN appeared in front of her eyes, and a stone swished above her head and crashed through a window, she panicked, backed suddenly, and was knocked down by a horse. Not even by a police horse. It was one of a pair of peaceful Whitbread's shire cart-horses that panicked as much as did she.

They took her directly to the mortuary. They thought they would find on her a card of the Women's Social and Political Union and the colours of the Union tied round her waist, but there was nothing of the sort. The only thing they found was her name and the name of the village. So they sent a telegram to her husband.

In the redbrick annexe glued to the side of Mr David D'Earth's (Sean's father's) thatched cottage, on the table in the recess of the bay window, stood a marvellous apparatus. The glistening fine brass, polished wood, electric wires. A long and narrow paper ribbon unwinding from a slowly revolving reel towards the inked nib which, push-pulled by two nervous electro-magnets, was pecking at the ribbon, dotting it with dots and dashing it with dashes. The village needed a little of everything, including a little of the late-nineteenth-century Progress. And Mr David D'Earth was a little of everything himself. Among other things, he was not only the Postmaster, he was also his own telegraphist.

There was no great demand for telegrams in the village. Not

every day was a day when one was sent or received, Mr D'Eath had had little opportunity to practise and would have found it difficult to code and decode them at great speed. But there was no need to hurry. And, at his own tempo, he was perfectly efficient and reliable. Yet, that morning, he found the message incomprehensible. Decipherable but incomprehensible. At first, it amused him. But a second later his heart missed a beat. The message contained a few words only, and three of those words were spelled DEATH:

—·· · ·— — ····

In Mr D'Eath's mind, the word *D'Eath* and the word *death* were situated in two separate compartments far away from each other. *D'Eath* was in the compartment containing such names as Roberts, Kitchener, Smuts, while *death* was on its own, alone. It was that tiniest typographical mite which people call *apostrophe* that kept them so far apart. Actually, there *was* a sign for it in the Morse Code. Alas, it was a cumbersome combination of dots and dashes ·— — — —· and the telegraph operators used to omit it, unless they were prudish, puritanical, pedantic perfectionists, and so it took him a long time to realize that the telegram was addressed —···— to himself, to him, Mr David D'EATH (spelled wrongly —·· · ·— — ···· instead of —·· ·— — — —· · ·— — ····), and that it was apprising him of the DEATH (spelled correctly —·· · ·— — ····) of his beloved wife, Mrs D'EATH (spelled wrongly —·· · ·— — ···· instead of —·· ·— — — —· · ·— — ····). He panicked. He ran across the road to the cottage of his friend Mr Pears, the Chemist; Mr Pears was already in his Pharmacy of course, but Mrs Pears was there, so he asked her to take care of Sean when he came back from school and, perhaps, put him up for the night if possible, he's such a sensitive boy; upon which he borrowed from her four pounds ten shillings six pence and three farthings which she collected from a vase in the kitchen, the leather purse in her handbag, and the pockets of her housecoat; 'God bless you,' he said, mounted his bicycle (actually it was a tandem with pneumatic tyres, the D'Eaths' wedding present), and pedalled some three miles to the railway station to catch the train to London.

In the middle of that night, in a strange bed in the spare room of Mr and Mrs Pears's cottage, Sean D'Eath woke up, pulled the blanket over his head and, keeping it above him like a tent, he knelt on the mattress, and said: 'Please, God, do make it not true. Please, God, tomorrow morning, do make the telegraph say it was a mistake.'

It was warm and dark and safe in the tent made from the blanket and yet an uneasy feeling began to grow on him. Perhaps there was not enough faith in his prayer? Perhaps it was more like testing God's power than like praying? Perhaps God couldn't hear him through the blanket? And if He did hear him, perhaps He didn't understand that he was hiding not from Him but from Mrs Pears, in case she came into the room. He yawned, stretched himself, and then curled up between the sheets and fell into a dreamless sleep.

He didn't go to school next morning. Mrs Pears made him a copious breakfast. 'Will you have *two* eggs and bacon and *two* little sausages, Sean?' she asked. And he said, 'Yes, please, Mrs Pears.' And then he said, 'Thank you, Mrs Pears.' And, as she wasn't sure what to do with him, 'Yes, to be sure, Sean. But do come back at lunch time,' she said when he asked her, 'May I go home now, Mrs Pears?'

He crossed the road. At that time of the morning, the maid (the gardener's daughter) should be there in the kitchen, the old postman (who had been walking twenty miles per day for the last forty years) should be sorting the mail collected from the railway station, and – who knows? – people might be coming to find out what had happened, the shoemaker who played second fiddle, the baker who played the bassoon, the butcher who played the clarinet? No door in the village was ever locked. There hadn't been any thieves in the village for as long as anyone remembered, and if a stranger came, a locked door would be a sign to him that there was nobody in the house, and so an invitation to break in. On the tips of his toes, to avoid meeting whoever might have been there (and whoever might have been there avoided him, perhaps), Sean went straight to the annexe with the bay window.

Nothing had changed. Everything was as his father had left it yesterday in a panic. Nothing new on the white tape hanging limply over the edge of the table. Nothing moved. He stood in front of it and tried to hypnotize the tape. Now was the time for God to send *dash dot dash dot dash* along the electric wire — · — · — *da di da di da* meaning: COME ON, ARE YOU READY TO RECEIVE MY MESSAGE? to which he, Sean, would answer *da di da* — · —, meaning: OK GOD, I'M READY, and then expect (¾ expect, ½ expect) God to say: YESTERDAY'S MESSAGE WAS · · · · · · · · (meaning *error*) ERASE IT!

After a minute (and a minute was a very long time for Sean) he suddenly thought that now he knew what it was to be grown up. To be grown up meant to stand in front of a motionless telegraphic apparatus knowing that one cannot *will* it to tick any dots and dashes.

During all that time, not once did he think of his mother. The fact that he would never see her again was so inconceivable that it wouldn't lodge in his mind. He looked once more at the shining brass, polished wood, and blank tape under the dead ink-writer, and with a shiver he realized that he had received no answer, not because his prayer wasn't good enough, but because there was no God to speak of.

•

He had found himself born into the kind of world in which the beauty of a telegraphic apparatus in a bay window was a natural part of everyday life, and this familiarity with it and with the Morse code (which he knew by heart from early childhood) brought him into prominence among his fellow wolf cubs.

At that time Sir (as he was then) Robert Baden-Powell's great vision of the Get-Up-And-Go-Scouting Movement, was rapidly being wrought into shape. One was already coming across some packs of 'little chaps in big hats and baggy shorts grasping staffs twice as tall as themselves' roaming about all over Sussex and Surrey. Sean was one of them. Patrol Leader Smith was another. But Patrol Leader Smith wasn't a wolf cub. Patrol Leader Smith was nearly twice Sean's age, and for Sean he was as grown up as real grown-ups; nevertheless, Patrol Leader Smith liked to talk to him, and Sean thought that to be singled out by somebody who could do and undo 58 knots, from the figure-of-eight knot to the French shroud knot, was indeed an honour.

'When you are twelve,' Smith said, as they were walking, pocket compass in hand, through the little wood they knew so well, 'or, maybe,' he continued, 'perhaps as a special favour when you are eleven, you'll be allowed to take an oath and you'll be a real scout then.'

For Sean to be twelve, or even to be eleven, was so unimaginably far away . . . Besides, there was that other thing Smith had said, and – he didn't know exactly why, but with some foreboding – Sean asked: 'Is one allowed to take an oath if one doesn't think much of God?'

'What?!' Smith stopped, stepped back and, as he was nearly twice as tall, looked down at Sean in astonishment. 'What did you say?'

'I mean, if one doesn't believe,' Sean said.

So far, nobody had spoken to him about his mother's death, and he hadn't told anybody about the NIGHT WHEN HE CHALLENGED GOD TO MAKE IT TO BECOME UNTRUE. That was his GREAT SECRET. It would have been nice, it would have been both relaxing and exciting to share that secret with somebody . . . Was Smith the right kind of person? Sean looked at him and decided not to say anything. Not now, anyway. Smith's face, seen from below, looked too stern. Smith was a good scout, and a good scout must show firmness of character. Firmness of character, yet without being obstinate or haughty. If in danger of losing his temper, he must count, silently, to ten or twenty, or thirty, to calm down. Smith counted, silently, to twenty. Then he decided to change the subject. From his shorts pocket he took out a pedometer, from his hip pocket he took out a ruler, from his side pocket a notebook, and from his breast pocket a pencil. He consulted the compass and the pedometer, put the notebook on Sean's shoulders, and drew a carefully measured triangle. Then he returned all these objects, except the compass, to their appropriate pockets, and said: 'We started walking north-east-by-north and we took 452 steps in that direction. Then we turned north-north-west and it took us 320 steps to get where we are now. I've calculated that if we go now south-by-west, it will take us 660 steps to get to the point we started from.'

They looked at the compass, turned south-by-west, started walking, and now Smith decided that he could tackle Sean's problem in a manner that was both fair and firm:

'To be an atheist,' he started in a calm lucid tone of voice, 'to be an unbeliever,' he added by way of explanation, 'is worse than to be Muslim, or a Hindu, or a Jew.' (He somehow omitted to say 'or a papist'.)

That was how Sean learnt the word *atheist* ·— — ····
· ·· ··· —.

Not sure that Sean had received the message, Smith, to emphasize what he had just said, repeated it, and he did so in reverse order:

'It is better to be a Jew, or a Hindu, or a Muslim, than to be an atheist,' he said.

'Why?' Sean asked.

Smith was quite prepared to answer this question. (After all, wasn't *Be prepared* the scout's watchword?)

'A good scout must be good, meaning ethical. And all ethics comes from God. Therefore a godless person cannot be ethical. He would be like an animal. Like that Mr Darwin's monkey. He would be rational. He would be asking for material reasons. And there is no material reason why one should be good rather than evil. Therefore, if you want to be a boy scout you must be good, and if you want to be good you must be religious, that's logic.' He consulted his pedometer and added, 'Another 348 steps and we'll arrive at our point of departure.'

That was how Sean learnt two more words: the word *ethics* · — ···· ·· —·—· ··· and the word *logic* ·—·· ——— ——· ·· —·—··. He was quite proud that Smith was speaking to him in such a grown-up way. And yet . . . Well, he admitted to himself, perhaps he was too young to grasp it, but Smith's words were rather confusing, because if *ethical* is *being good* then why did Smith say that Mr Darwin's monkey cannot be ethical? And who was that Mr Darwin anyway? A zoo keeper? Was it only his, Mr Darwin's, monkey that wasn't ethical, or did Smith mean that all monkeys are not ethical, which is not quite what he, Sean, felt, because what about that big monkey they call ape, the she-ape whose photograph was printed in the *National Geographic Magazine*, didn't she look so very ethical there as she held a little baby-ape in her arms and caressed and deloused it so sweetly, and . . . Suddenly he blushed; suddenly a thought about his own mother came to him, his own mother who had been killed not so long ago and he already couldn't remember what she looked like, and – suddenly – he felt as if he was betraying her because he remembered the photograph of the she-ape so much better and was even envying the little baby-ape who was so *ethically* caressed by the big she-ape, and so he blushed and looked up to see whether Smith had noticed, but he obviously had not, luckily. 'I do like to talk to you, D'Eath,' he said, and then, for some reason or other, he added 'anyway', and Sean didn't know what the reason was, but whatever it was, he didn't like it, he didn't know why, but he didn't, and they were already standing by the little bridge over the stream, the very place from which they had started their walk, and Smith said, 'Well, be prepared. *Dib dib dib*,' and he saluted, and not waiting for Sean to say *dob dob dob*, Smith marched off.

Sean would have liked to tell Smith everything, everything about his thoughts. But he knew that he had not enough grown-up words to express them. All he had just learnt was *atheist*, *ethics*, and *logic*. That, he felt, was not enough. Especially as he wasn't quite sure – did he understand them correctly? Smith had said *ethics* and *ethical*, but could one say *to ethic*? As one says, for instance, *to kill*, or *to eat*? It would be much easier if one could. One would be able to say: the great ape sits and ethics. Smith said that animals cannot be ethical. Why not, if they do ethic, and they do, don't they? Doesn't the big mother-ape ethic? Don't birds (except for the cuckoo, perhaps) when they sit on their eggs instead of eating them for breakfast? Doesn't even the fox ethic, even when he kills and steals a chicken to take it to his vixen and their little foxes? So perhaps there are two ethics. One is the big she-ape's ethics based on ethicking, the other is Smith's ethics based on commanding. He, Sean, felt he was much further from Smith than he, Sean, was from the big she-ape, and that he was much closer to her because she and he knew what it was to ethic, though neither of them knew how to express it, how to express it in words. Grown-up people have no idea how many thoughts, what heavy thoughts, what great thoughts, what important thoughts, what true thoughts a wolf cub may have without being able to express them in words, which is strange, very strange, because grown-ups must also have been little boys or little girls once upon a time, so how is it that they don't remember? He, Sean, will never forget . . . Never forget what? Well, his great Thoughts, great Truth, great Discovery! What discovery? What truth? What thoughts? Well, how can he say it if those things are wordless, as wordless, as wordless as those of the big she-ape caressing her baby, as those of the couple of pigeons sitting on their eggs, as those of the fox stealing the chicken, how can he, Sean, say it if he doesn't know the right words, it's so strange, so mysterious, to have those Thoughts in you and not be able to pin them down with words, it's frightening, his whole body feels tense, uncomfortable under his big hat, under his blouse, even in his baggy shorts, so many thoughts are gathering together like clouds, and they are all about what Smith called 'ethics', and about what the big she-ape does, and it is so that it is precisely because she does it that she *is*, and her baby is, and he (Sean) is, and everything is, not like the dodo, because the dodo didn't, the dodo stopped doing it, the dodo stopped ethicking, and that's how it disappeared, got extinct, because to ethic is . . . No, he, Sean, doesn't know how to say it. 'Damn it all!' (that was the *swearest* word his father would utter), 'Damn it all!' he repeated and he took a stone and threw it into the stream, and he repeated, 'Damn it' once again, and he threw another stone, and his thoughts disappeared in the same way as the two stones disappeared under the water, they disappeared and the world was again peaceful and beautiful, they disappeared but he knew that they did not vanish, not for ever, they were still in him, submerged, and they had remained thus submerged, mutely, unnamed, wordless, for the next sixty years, till the evening of the day when his own son, Adam, came (as he used to, once a week, since Sean D'Earth retired), and said: 'Father, I've got a new job.'

'Will you like it?'

'Yes, I think I will. In a way.'

'Well then, that's fine. What is it?'

His son hesitated.

'I'm afraid I can't tell you much about it. It's classified.'

'Oh . . .' Sean D'Earth said.

•

By the end of the war (the Second Great War) a homosexual fighter pilot from Alabama fell desperately in love with Prickly Rose who regarded it as a point of honour that she'd succeed in converting him to heterosexual normality. She did. And soon after · · · —  V for Victory · · · —

V-Day, they both flew to his beloved Alabama and vanished from sight.

For Sean, it was good riddance. He deplored the fact that the boy had been left by his mother, but on the other hand he enjoyed having him all to himself. His burden became the purpose of his life. His Prickly Rose was forgiven and forgotten, all thoughts about the other woman, the pretty young lady in uniform (who in the meantime had got married, had a child, and lost her husband) were put into the private, locked compartment of his remembrance. All that counted now was his stockbroking and little Adam. And when the boy proved to be so good at mathematics and physics at school, Sean was overjoyed. Which needs to be explained.

Some pedants maintain that the twentieth century begins on the 1st of January 1901 and therefore the whole year and thirty minutes, and not a mere half hour of the life of Sean (who was born at thirty minutes to midnight on the 31st December 1899) belonged to the nineteenth century, and a nineteenth-century atheist either thinks that History is Science and everything is basically explainable, or he is struck by the Mystery of the Universe, the Mystery of Existence, and thinks that the physical sciences, empirical researches, are the tools that can help us to peer into the dark corners of the mystery and see a flicker of light. No, not in the vain hope of solving the Unsolvable by reducing it to philosophical atomic smithereens. Nor of dissolving it in the sweet smell of incense. But just to approach it, just a little, by helping us to shake off some inherited beliefs that impair our judgement. Because the less of such prejudiced beliefs we have, the nearer we are to the truth, even if it is never finally obtainable. Thus, for the nineteenth-century atheist, Science, the capital S science, was *the* thing. The New Science. Astrophysics. Physico-chemistry. Molecular Biology.

That was why he (who limited his own activities to buying and selling for clients stocks held by stock jobbers) rejoiced when his son proved to be good at mathematics and physics at school; and when, later on, he was found to be so brilliant at the Imperial College of Technology and became a genuine research scientist, Sean D'Earth felt as proud as only a peasant woman can be proud when her son is ordained a priest.

What had been the purpose of his life was fulfilled. The beautiful picture of what had been achieved was there, ready to be looked at. Who would believe that it could be torn to pieces in a second, the long second during which Sean D'Earth said, 'Oh . . .' and his heart missed a beat, when his son told him about his new job, the classified job?

'In a way, it's all your doing, Father. Those things are logical consequences of what *you* are for. You are for nuclear disarmament. All right. Then we must develop our conventional weapons, mustn't we? Mustn't we be prepared?'

But Sean D'Earth knew that the real game was played elsewhere. Sean D'Earth, the retired stockbroker, born at the end of the last century, looked at his son, the scientist, born into the Labour Government's world of the Welfare State, brought up on its 1945 free milk and orange juice – and was puzzled.

Who do they think they are, his own son and all those scientists who want us to be prepared?

The saviours of civilization?

Do they think mothers will point them out to their children saying: 'Look, darling, there goes Professor Adam D'Earth who has loaded his missile with something so marvellous that it will make your blinded eyes radiate in all their glory for the next 30,000 years; – run up to him, my darling, make him a curtsey, and give him this bunch of poppies.'

41

Or: 'Look, darling, there goes Dr Fieser who's managed to mix naphthalene with coconut and made a lovely jelly that will stick to you as it burns and make you into the beautiful Olympic torch of Liberty; – run, my darling, curtsey to him, and give him this bunch of cornflowers.'

Or: 'Look, darling, there goes Academician Andrei Dimitryevich Sakharov who has developed a hydrogen bomb that is going to kill you; – run up to him, my darling, hurry up, and – before he goes mad – give him these lilies of the valley.'

Suddenly, so many things around him began to look different. His son was no longer an atheist priest celebrating the Mysteries of the Universe; the wallpaper in his room acquired an intricate fractal pattern he had never noticed before; and then – since that day of *'Oh . . .'* – even people in the street . . . yes, what was the matter with them? What *is* the matter with them? Why do they look at him, look at him and then, quickly, turn their eyes away?

He touches all his buttons and zips – they are in their right places. When he comes back home, he goes straight to the mirror - nothing seems to be wrong: he's six foot tall, well dressed, well . . . correctly dressed, as always, his moustache is trimmed, his shoes are polished, he doesn't see anything strikingly wrong in his appearance, and yet, all this is not just his imagination, he doesn't imagine things, people *do* look at him and then turn away, they look askance at him and then turn away embarrassed, Why?, he wonders, Oh dear . . . maybe it isn't what they see. But what else? Is it his smell? Old people don't smell their own smell. *Anosmia patialis.* And nobody would dare mention it to them. Of course they wouldn't. Perhaps that Xmas present, that box of sandalwood soap he was given last Xmas, perhaps it was a hint . . . So that was that, that must have been why that silly woman said, 'Fuck off!' when she walked past him in the street the other day, not long ago. Unless it was because she could read his thoughts. Though they had nothing to do with *her*. He remembered her well. She was coming towards him. Smoking a cigarette. Drunk? Or drugged? What age was she? Could have been his daughter. Could have been his granddaughter. Easily. Walked straight towards him and, passing by, said those two words precisely at the moment when he was thinking about the big she-ape and her baby, which had nothing to do with the woman, the picture of the she-ape and child had already been in him for some time, perhaps for a long time, he wasn't sure, but it certainly was there also at the moment he said, 'Oh . . .' and his heart missed a beat when his son told him about his new *classified* job – just conjured itself out of nothing, such a vivid picture of a she-ape and child, nothing to do with the woman who passed him in the street, a beautiful picture, like pictures of the Madonna, Raphael's pictures of the Madonna, the Madonna and Child, that's it, warm Renaissance Madonnas, not those stiff Byzantine frightening Mothers, no; when did he first see such a beautiful Renaissance She-ape and Child?, he couldn't remember, but she was there, in his inner eye, smiling to her baby and saying, 'Be prepared!', and so he walked (because he was a great walker) and thought (because he had become a great thoughter) and so he walked and thought, Why do they print photographs of monkeys in books on Darwin but never in books on Marx? And even in those books on Darwin, what they print are Byzantine skeleton-monkeys, there is no Renaissance pink warmth in them, and really why do those people, why do they not see that it is this warm She-ape and Child's · — ···· ·· —·—· ··· that is at the base of · ···— — —— ·—·· ··— — ·· ——— —· ··—··.

He would walk in the streets of South London and North London, up river towards Richmond and down river to the extinct docks of London, he would park his car anywhere, write on a scrap of paper the name of the place, as he had no more confidence in his memory, and he would walk and think. Why do they not see that it is precisely what they are afraid to call *the ape's ethics* that is at the base of what they call *evolution*, because, isn't it so?, isn't it so that without her being · — ···· ·· —·—· ·— ·—·· there would be not a single ape to · ···— — — — ·—·· ···—·. The old boy-scout habit of practising the Morse code came back to him. Why? he asked.

didada didididi dadidada

Some passers-by might have given him a glance of embarrassment or compassion, but he had already checked all his buttons and his zip-fasteners and would march on, musing, finding great pleasure in turning his thoughts into words, the same thoughts once more, and again and again, well, yes, granted, the lion doesn't eat straw like an ox, he eats the ox and what remains he gives to his cubs; and the foxes, they spoil the vines, and steal the chicken and bring it to their holes among the lilies to feed the little foxes, but is it just to feed Deborah that his son, her father, invents, and designs, and blue-prints those things that are then tested in Vietnam, in Afghanistan, in the Middle East? There is no Hippocratic oath for scientists. His son, Adam, is not a scientist of life. His son, Adam, is a scientist of death. And yet, suddenly – death or no death – he realized how much he loved his son. He would hate what his son was doing but he couldn't stop loving him. Just because he was his son. For no other reason. And that was precisely *the* thing that had made the omnivorous animal, man and beast, tick over the eons, the very thing that had made the she-ape fit to survive as a species, that chemistry of love contained in a bit of DNA which we are born with; yes, indeed, that's where the real game is played. Isn't it? Your verdict, gentlemen. How say you?

'Are you talking to me, sir? Can I help you?' a young man with a tennis racket was standing in front of him.

'What? What's that?' It took Sean a long while to catch on and see what had happened. 'No,' he said. 'Thank you. Must have been talking to myself. Gone crazy, I presume.'

'I didn't hear what you were saying, sir, but it sounded as if it could have been a poem.'

'Very kindly put,' Sean said. 'Very kindly, indeed.'

The young man hesitated, but finding no encouragement to proceed, he awkwardly saluted the old man with his tennis racket and bolted.

So that was that! Now he knew. The mystery was solved. No unbuttoned buttons, no unzipped zips, no *anosmia patialis*, no readings of thoughts, but just an old man walking in the street and talking to himself, out loud. No wonder the woman said 'fuck off' if 'the big she-ape' was what she had overheard. 'Oh, dear me!' He had thought that such things as talking to oneself in the street happen only to other people. And now it had happened to him. He must stop it. He must shut up. He did. But now, when he stopped talking, his thoughts had become unbearably heavy. Unbearably. Like the thoughts of a child who went into tantrums because of a dearth of words that could express them. So he stopped thinking. He was just gaping.

•

'How are you, Father?'

'What? Oh yes. I'm fine, my boy. Fine.' He didn't like to be called 'Father'. But he didn't know that his son didn't like to be called 'my boy'. There had been many things they didn't know about each other.

'I'm sorry I'm late, Father. The blasted traffic.'

'Not at all, not at all, my boy. And you are not late. Not late at all. I only came back myself minutes before you.'

'You haven't been driving?'

'No. 'M not using my car much now. Prefer walking.'

'Walking doesn't tire you?'

'Not in the least. Can walk for miles. Find it very healthy.'

'Good.'

Then they were talking about milk. Milk in bottles and milk in cartons. Advantages and disadvantages of two different methods of packaging. If one were to ask them, later on, what it was that made them embark on this subject, they wouldn't remember.

A black-bordered printed card was lying on the coffee table between them.

'Nothing special happened since I saw you last, Father?'

He opened his mouth to speak, he wanted to say: Yes, I have discovered that I have been talking to myself in the street. But he closed his mouth and then opened it again and said, casually: 'Does the name Lady Cooper mean anything to you?'

'Lady Diana Cooper?'

'No. Nothing to do with her. The late Sir Lionel's widow.'

'I'm afraid not. Why?'

'She has died,' he said. 'I forgot that she used to drink gin and tonic and I thought it was a *non sequitur*,' he remarked cryptically.

'Oh,' his son said. Then he thought that perhaps she had been one of his father's lady friends, and he added, 'I'm sorry.'

'I met her first the day you were born, my boy.'

He pushed the black-bordered card nearer to his son.

'Oh, must be Perceval's mother. I know him, of course, we were at school together. He was much younger. We used to torment him a lot. Rather. Now he is in some sort of Health Farm racket.'

But Sean D'Earth didn't want to talk about Perceval and his Health Farm. He wanted to talk about Bukumla. Bukumla? Why Bukumla? Never mind why. He wanted to talk about Bukumla but not with his son. There was a revolution in Bukumla, and mentioning Bukumla now would make them talk politics, and talking politics would make them quarrelsome, so, instead of asking about Bukumla, he said: 'But what about you, my boy? Tell me about yourself. How's Lucy? How's everything?'

Shyly avoiding his eye, Dr D'Earth said: 'As a matter of fact, there's something I've not told you about yet. But I don't know how you'll take it. I'm going to be knighted . . .'

'Oh . . . ! That's great. Congratulations. You'll be Sir Adam D'Earth. Your grandfather would have been delighted.'

'Which grandfather?'

'Which what?!'

'I understand I had two grandfathers.'

'You mean your mother's father? He would have been delighted too, I'm sure.'

'You never tell me about Mother. As if I hadn't had one.'

'I don't know, my boy. I don't know, Son. She must be a very old lady now, if she's still alive.'

'You've never divorced?'

'No.'

'So she couldn't have remarried, could she? And if she had some children, they would be bastards, wouldn't they?'

'Unless those things could have been arranged without me, in Reno, or somewhere . . .'

'You think they could?'

'I don't know, Son. Haven't heard from her since she left.'

'The man's name was Hobson, wasn't it? Like Hobson's choice.'

'Yes. It was. But why? What's on your mind, Son?'

'Nothing. Just a coincidence. Life is full of coincidences. Isn't it?'

'Nothing annoying about it, I hope. Nothing to do with your knighthood?'

'No, Father. Nothing to do with my bloody knighthood that everybody is so delighted with. Everybody, except just one person I would like to be.'

'You mean your mother?'

'Mother? What mother? I never thought I had a mother.'

47

'You can't mean me, Son. I *am* glad. In my own way.'

'Of course not, Father. I don't mean you. I mean my own daughter.'

'Deborah?'

'Well, she's the only daughter I have, isn't she?'

'I adore Deborah.'

'I know you do, Father. I know you *adore* Deborah who turns her nose up at everything that concerns me.' Suddenly, his voice changed. And his vocabulary changed. He sounded now as if he were talking to a microphone, addressing some parliamentary committee . . . 'I'm sorry you don't disapprove of her disdainful superiority and arrogance which I resent. My daughter Deborah! Deborah, the poet. I wish you'd hear her obscenities and see her outrageous outfit and make-up!'

It was the tone of his voice that made Sean D'Earth decide not to tell him that he had just seen Deborah, that very afternoon, just a few hours ago.

•

He was glad he hadn't told his son about meeting Deborah. The day was already full enough of events that wouldn't lead anywhere. Or would they? It had started with the postman who brought him that black-edged card saying that Lady Cooper was dead and buried. It took his brain a moment or two to 'process' the information. Anyway, that's how his son would have described it. Lady Cooper was no more. He hadn't seen her for many years, yet it was good, it was natural to know that she was there, though unseen, in the landscape that surrounded him. Now the landscape had changed. At his age, one had seen the trees growing and the heart didn't need to turn to travel, by land or by water, to see new scenery. Travelling in time alone shifts the scenes, moves the new props in and the old cast out.

He went out, closing the door behind him. The door

48

squeaked. He took the key from his pocket, opened the door, fetched a little oilcan from the shelf in the loo, oiled the hinges, took the oilcan back, opened the door, closed it noiselessly and went for a stroll. A stroll? No. It was not going to be just a stroll. There was an intent. A purpose. What purpose? Never mind. One doesn't need to carry one's purpose in front of one's nose in order to know in which direction to go. He knew where to go. Along the Canal, towards Paddington Station.

He liked the old Paddington Station. Kingdom Brunel. Great Western Railway. Et cetera. His senses still expected to smell the smell of hot iron and steam, and to hear the locomotive engines slowing down at the arrival platforms, and the accelerated puff puff puff of those departing westwards.

He left the station through the lobby of the Great Western Royal Hotel. He knew that he should turn left now and go up Praed Street. But what for? The word was on the tip of his tongue, but . . . when alone in the street, he was obsessed by the fear that, once he allowed his thoughts to become words, he'd start talking to himself again. And that must never happen again. No. He'll not turn left now. He'll go straight on. There's no hurry. He'll leave the purpose for a little while. He'll leave it submerged. Perhaps on his way back he'll turn into Praed Street and the purpose will emerge by itself.

He went straight on. Towards the park. Hyde Park. Victoria Gate. Too many cars were streaming in and out through Victoria Gate. He turned right and walked along the Bayswater Road to Marlborough Gate and through it to Kensington Gardens.

No clouds between the midday sun above and the green trees down here. Peter Pan on his right. The Serpentine on his left. Big birds sailing unhurriedly on the surface of the water, little birds jumping among the branches of the trees, people strolling relaxedly. Chirp. Chirp. Chirp. That was a man, a big, solid, burly man chirruping. A slice of bread high above his head, chirp chirp chirp, and the sparrows would alight to nibble at it. And he looked up towards the sparrows dancing above him, and there was a smile on his big face.

Sean D'Earth sat on the bench opposite to look at him. And then he closed his eyes and saw another man approaching. And that other man was small, and he was wearing a heavy and shabby winter overcoat, as if it was his only possession, *omnia mea mecum porto*, as if in this sultry weather he nowhere had a hanger to hang it on, and he, the small man, approached the big man who was feeding the sparrows, and said, 'Let me do it,' and the big man gave him a slice from a plastic carrier bag full of bread, and the small man put the slice of bread into his mouth, upon which the big man gripped him by the throat and shouted, 'Spit it out! Spit it out, you fool. Don't you know the bread is poisoned?!' and the small man spat it out and gave a groan of despair and fear, and ran away retching, and the big man turned to the bench and said, 'What a fool, there's no poison in my bread, to be sure; what sort of man would poison the little sparrows?' and then Sean D'Earth opened his eyes, and everything was as it was before, the big, solid, burly man holding a slice of bread high above his head and chirp chirp chirp smiling to the sparrows. But what Sean D'Earth had seen when his eyes were closed was much more vivid than what he now saw with his eyes wide open. That moment of his vision was stronger than reality. 'Good God,' he said, not noticing that he had said it aloud. 'Good God,' he repeated, frightened that the memory of what he saw with his eyes open might tomorrow, or tomorrow week, or month, or year, be erased and only the memory of what he saw with his eyes closed would remain as the memory of what really had happened. Was it so easy to shift the burden of life from the world of reality to the world of fantasy? He got up and marched off to have some food.

•

## D'Eath into D'Earth

The road winding its way from Victoria Gate, Bayswater, to Alexandra Gate, Knightsbridge, and thus cutting the Park in halves, swarmed with motorcars, horses and ponies ridden by little girls and small boys, their faces so pensive and solemn.

Sean D'Earth recrossed the road on his way back from the restaurant where he just had a grilled Dover sole and a glass of wine and nothing else, and then a black coffee and a brandy and nothing else. They knew him there and liked him. They put him at a table by the window with a view over that long curving lake that longs to be called a river, which once upon a time it used to be, and they didn't mind his leaving a miserly tip – to be sure, the old gentleman was still living in the world of £.s.d. and had an exaggerated feeling about the value of a white metal coin.

He loved the Park and its trees. He thought they were the most beautiful trees in the world. Except perhaps those in the little wood in the village where he was born. There, the leaves were greener, and the smells were stronger, and the breeze was gentler, and one could have a pee against a tree trunk. He had already had a pee a short while ago in the restaurant's loo, but (and he hoped it had nothing to do with his prostate) he felt the urge to empty his bladder again. There was a path among the trees leading to a white pavilion, an art gallery – he hoped there might be a loo there. There was. There were also some pictures on the walls, which he hadn't noticed. But he did look at the strange objects displayed *par terre* outside the pavilion. A sculpture made of welded, rolled and hammered sheets of iron which a scrap-metal man had offered to remove without payment; an upside down periscope, so cleverly buried in the earth that when you looked down into a hole in the ground, you saw the faraway view of the rowing boats and the sky above them; and then there were two Madame Tussaud life-size figures lying on the lawn, side by side. The male figure was clad in what looked like some theatrical outfit, reminiscent of *La Belle Époque*? *Fin de Siècle*?

(the nineteenth century '*siècle*', of course). The female figure was perhaps meant to be punk, or post-punk, or neo-punk, or what else? Its shoes, one red one yellow, stood separately beside its feet, like two stuffed birds fixed to the green grass. Sean D'Earth walked twice round them, wondering what they were made of: wax or what's called fibreglass, well, wax should have started melting by now, in that scorching sun. Was that what the artist wanted, some sort of surrealism? How awful! Inhuman! But maybe they are not wax, maybe they are fibreglass, but what is that fibreglass exactly? He stretched the index finger of his right hand, bent forward, and was moving it nearer to the big toe of the female dummy. At that moment the male dummy opened its eyes.

'Good God! My abject apologies!' Sean D'Earth said. 'I thought you were modern sculptures . . .'

Now the female figure jumped to her feet: 'Grandpasean!' (she pronounced 'sean' as if it was '*chon*' in French) 'What are you doing here? How splendid! Great!'

'Deborah . . . !' Sean D'Earth exclaimed.

'This is my grandfather. Sean D'Earth,' Deborah said. 'And this is John St Austell, Bernard St Austell's son. I'm sure you . . .'

'I knew your father. And I think I saw you when you were a schoolboy,' Sean said.

'He doesn't like to be known as his famous father's son,' Deborah said. 'He's even changed his name to Austel, which he spells Ostel, which I think is a silly thing to do because it sounds like *hostel* and, besides, nobody today remembers the name of that Great Man of Letters, his father. Not anybody of my age, anyway.' She turned to the young man and said, 'John, this is a special occasion. I want to have my Grandpasean all to myself. Be an angel, go and look at the pictures, and don't come back till I call you.' She took her grandfather gently by the elbow and led him to the nearby bench.

'Sir . . .' the young man said, haltingly, and moved away.

'Grandpasean, how marvellous to see you! Great! Absolutely! Oh shit! Oh fuck!' she exclaimed. She was barefoot. She had left her one red shoe and one yellow shoe on the grass, and now two cuddling pigeons were trying to fit themselves into them. She shoed the birds away, put on the shoes and came back to sit beside Sean on the bench. 'You must tell me what you know about John, Grandpasean. I know that you know a lot about him. And I don't know a thing. I mean – about his past. When I ask him, he just clams up. All I know is what people say. Gossip. As for me, I don't care. I mean, I take him as he is. But there is a special reason, a very special reason why I must know something about his past. Is it true what people say? First, that he was mad, certified mad. Then, that he used to be a policeman. And then, that he made millions by buying and selling houses? He doesn't seem to have those millions now. How much truth is there in all that, Grandpasean?'

He didn't like the elaborate bald patches shaved on her head. He didn't like her trousers, one leg in one colour the other in another; one narrow, the other wide, like a skirt. He didn't like the asymmetry of it. But he liked her. Dear Deborah. Was that how she was trying to express her soul? Her delayed, revolting scream against the severance of her umbilical cord? Her navel?

Thy navel is like a round goblet, which wanteth not liquor; thy belly is like an heap of wheat set about with lilies.

He blushed. No, it isn't done to think about one's granddaughter's navel, is it? Even if she tried to express it as if it were her soul. As all those young poets . . . the navel, that's where poetry is to be found, conceived, and composed, the navel, or below it, that's what they think. By contemplating their own navel, they express their soul, that's what they believe. Ha ha. As for him, Sean D'Earth, he would never try to express his soul. Goodness me, no! Not even to himself.

53

His soul was his own personal thing. He kept it jealously to himself and for himself. Whatever it was. Without dissecting it. He felt that expressing it would mean losing it. No longer having it. Because one loses what one expresses. One loses things by expressing them. And he didn't want to lose his soul. Not even a little bit of it. No, not a bit. And now it occurs to him that perhaps she too – oh dear me! – perhaps things are not so simple . . . Perhaps she's trying to get rid of what is *not* her soul, perhaps she's trying to find her soul by trying to get rid of what is not *it*?

'Well . . . ?'

'What?'

'You promised to tell me, Grandpasean. It's important for me to know. Not only for my sake. Or for his. It's important for the sake of Mother.'

'His mother?'

'No!' she said. 'For the sake of my mother, Lucy, for the sake of her job. Don't you see, Grandpasean?'

He didn't see but he didn't say that he didn't. If it was so important for John's mother, he would understand. He knew John's mother. And he knew John's father. The Great Man of Letters. So long ago. How funny . . . He used to be the Great Man's stockbroker, and of that he managed not to remember a thing. A blank, my Lord. Blank. Suddenly, however, just now, on the background of that blank, a tableau vivant from the past . . . The country house of the Great Man of Letters. So serene. On that brilliant summer day. And he, Sean D'Earth is there. Invited to lunch? He doesn't remember. But it doesn't matter. What he remembers, so vividly, is the door. He's opening the door to the drawing room. He just starts opening the door, and stops. The Great Man and his son, John, are in the drawing room. They don't see him. But he sees them. And, somehow, he feels that it would be wrong to burst in, and impossible to retreat without making a sound. He stands still. Ajar with himself. Sweating. And the son, John, says something like ' . . . well, Dad, it's rather difficult to say, because I disagree with you . . .' And the Great Man says, very courteously, 'We are all entitled to our own opinions.' And the son says, 'Well, Dad, I read what you wrote about . . .' But the Great Man interrupts him: 'No, Son, I do *not* wish to discuss my work . . .' And the son says, 'But why . . . ?' And the Great Man says, 'I do not wish to discuss my reasons either,' and he gets up and leaves the room through the garden door, fortunately. And now John is all alone in the room and the room is filled with heavy hatred. The air in the room is saturated with it. Can hatred really be a physical phenomenon? Do some pheromones of it really exist? Can they be detected by some physical gadgets? Like some odd electrons can be detected when the air is ionized by a faraway thunderstorm and the induced charge on your hair makes it stand on end? He retreats, silently. And he feels guilty. Should he be leaving the boy all by himself in that drawing room that has lost its serenity? Well, all that happened so long ago. The boy, John St Austell, who calls himself now John Ostel, must have been fifteen or sixteen at the time. Still, it was some years after he, Sean D'Earth, retired. So his visit to the country house must have been a social visit. Not a business visit. Though he didn't claim that he and the Great Man of Letters were close friends. Well, let's say – just friends. And when, not long after that visit, the Great Man of Letters died, so suddenly, on the floor of a little railway station between his village and London, and his widow, Anne, went to Majorca with Marjorie, his secretary, to settle there with her for good, she still kept in touch with him, asking for advice on family matters, sending him Christmas cards, and remembering his birthday. And one day she phoned him from Majorca and asked, 'Is it you, Sean?'

and he said, 'Yes . . .'

and she said, 'I'm going to ask you a question, Sean,'

and he said, 'Yes?'

and she said, 'What do you think of Samuel Beckett?'

and he said, 'What?!'

and . . .

'Wake up, Grandpasean,' Deborah said. 'You've promised to tell me . . .'

'I *am* telling you, am I not?'

'No, you aren't,' Deborah said.

'Well, I thought I had just told you that she phoned me one day from Majorca, and . . .'

'Who phoned you from Majorca?' Deborah asked.

'Anne. The Great Man's widow. John's mother. Of course.'

'And?' Deborah asked.

'Well, she phoned me from Majorca and asked what I thought of Samuel Beckett.'

'What?!' Deborah asked.

'That's precisely what I said. "What?!" And so she said she had just heard that her son, John, was going mad. He had been told to write a thesis on Samuel Beckett. For his degree. And reading Samuel Beckett had affected his health and he was heading for a nervous breakdown. So I told her that if a young man becomes depressed by reading Samuel Beckett, that very fact proves that he's perfectly sane. But she said that I didn't understand what she had said. She said she had been told that he had been driven really mad. Bonkers. Round the bend. And could I do something about it, or must she fly from Majorca to Scotland where his university was? So I said I'd try. And I got in touch with his tutor. And told him not to be an ass. And he agreed to change the subject of John's thesis from Samuel Beckett to Flann O'Brien, and John at once recovered from that brainstorm or whatever it was, and got his degree, and he doesn't know that it cost me a case of good claret for the tutor, and that's all there is in what they tell you about his being mad. It's not true. But not entirely untrue. And it's the same about his being a policeman. Not true. But not entirely untrue. And if you hear that he became a policeman to help his sister to be spirited away, that's just silly!'

'His sister?' Deborah asked.

'Didn't you know he had a sister?'

'No, I didn't. What about her?'

'Oh dear me. Nobody knows exactly . . . It could have been CND. It could have been an Arab boyfriend. Or Irish. It could have been any combination of Crime and Idea. But what that particular crime was and that particular idea – nobody knows exactly. All one knows is that she's been spirited away. Her mother thinks she's now with some guru in India. But none of this has anything to do with John's being or not being a policeman.'

'Now, Grandpa . . . that's precisely what I must know. Is he a policeman? Has he ever been a policeman? Yes or no?' she asked, and waited for an answer.

'My sweet love,' he said. 'You write poems. Are not poets the very people who know that no truth can be found by asking *yes or no*? Nothing in this world is just *yes or no*, is it? Isn't it?' He paused, and then said quickly, 'All right, my dear. I'll tell you all I know. When John got his degree, he came to London to celebrate. I know because very early in the morning I had a telephone call from Paddington Green Police Station asking, Do I know so-and-so? You see, John would never write to me or come to see me, but whenever he was asked for a reference or a testimonial, he would give my name and address, which pleased me, it meant he had confidence in me. And so, you see, Deborah, that was how I heard what had happened. He came to London to celebrate his degree. Must have had quite a few pints of ale and, late at night, walking along Edgware Road, of all places, he felt a sudden urge to empty his bladder. As there was, apparently, no loo anywhere, and all the pubs were already closed, he turned into a side street, stood in a dark niche in front of a padlocked door, and unzipped, or unbuttoned, when a heavy hand fell on his shoulder. Two policemen were standing behind him. The shock was such that his vesical sphincter contracted and he was unable to demonstrate his reasons for being where he was, and so they accused him of trying what they called "to break and enter", took him to the police station where he spent the night, and then to the court. As no tools had been found on him, they changed the charge to that of vagrancy, for which he was duly fined. You know him, Deborah, so you can imagine how he must have fumed with rage. But he was a romantic. He thought the police are rotten not because they are rotten on principle, but because they only recruit bloody conservative bullies instead of such decent, intelligent, educated people as himself. So he joined them. Yes, he did. As a trainee, I suppose. So that's a bit of your truth. It didn't last long. Less than a year later, I got a letter from some estate agents asking for a testimonial. So, obviously, he must have left the Force and got himself a job buying and selling houses, as you said, but I don't know for sure, haven't heard from him since. What is he doing now? You should know.'

'He's in films,' Deborah said.

'What sort of films?'

'Short films.'

'Is that where you met him?'

'Sort of . . .'

He wanted to say *I see* . . . But he didn't.

'He's a Greek scholar,' she added quickly. 'He has translated some Sappho. Beautifully.'

Now he did say, 'I see . . .'

—.—.  —..  —.—..

dadi dadi dadidi dadi dadi

His mind translated the Sapphic stanza into the Morse code, though he was not aware of it.

—..  —..

People walking on the lawn in front of the Gallery were pretending that they were not showing that they were pretending not to see them. Darting suspicious looks at the old gentleman and scornful glances at the outrageously costumed girl. Punk? Post-punk? Neo-punk? What could such a pair have in common? Sitting there on the bench and talking. What can they be talking about?

But they were not talking at that moment. They were looking straight into each other's eyes. As if it were a game. Whose eyes would blink first? His did.

'Tell me what happened,' he said. 'Why did you say that it is for the sake of your mother that you must know all those things about John?'

Her eyes still looked straight into him. But now she smiled. 'Actually,' she said, 'so far,' she added, 'it has nothing to do with John. Mother doesn't even know him.'

'Well then?' he asked.

'Well,' she repeated after him, 'Mother is going on one of her hush-hush missions or whatever it is. And she wants to take me with her. On condition that I dress properly and am a good girl. It sounds exciting. By helicopter to some sort of a desert island. I'm tempted to go and I don't mind dressing properly and being a good girl, but I want to take John with us. That's why I asked you about him. Because, you see, if he really has anything to do with the police, politics, that sort of thing, then it is off. Absolutely. Because it would be risky for Mother. For her job. And I don't want to do anything that could embarrass her. Absolutely not. Even if I don't think much of what she does. I mean, even if I don't know much of what her job is.' She paused, and then started in a different tone of voice. 'You know, Grandpasean, it's rather *weird* to have *two* hush-hush parents. Well, yes, Mother's being hush-hush about her job, I sort of understand. Maybe it runs in the family. Wasn't *her* mother one of those upper-class young ladies slaving patriotically in that Codes and Ciphers establishment at Bletchley Park during the war? But Father? Why Father? He's a scientist. Why does he say nothing about his job, as if he were ashamed of it? Has he too got a mother complex? Who was she? I mean *his* mother? Why has nobody ever told me anything about her? Is it true that people called her a Prickly Rose?'

'Yes, they did,' he said.

'And what has happened to her?'

'I don't know, my dear. I haven't heard from her since she left me.'

'It was she who left *you?*'

'Yes, it was.'

'Was it very awful for you, Grandpasean?'

'Oh no,' he said. 'On the contrary . . . it was rather . . . h'm . . . euphoric. Actually, I would have left my Prickly Rose long before she left me, if it hadn't been for the baby. You see, I, myself, I lost my mother when I was a little boy. And so I thought that a baby must have a mother.'

'A baby?' she asked. 'What baby?'

'Your father, my dear . . .'

It took her a moment or two to catch on. And then she said, 'Fuck! I never thought that pompous ass of a father of mine could ever have been a baby!'

They both laughed. Not in unison. Theirs were two different kinds of laughter. A little dog on the lawn must have liked the sound of it. 'Wooff wooff,' it barked gaily, as if to join them, and started chasing its tail.

'Well, I have told you all I know about John,' he said. 'Can you decide now what to do? Are you going to ask Lucy to invite him?'

'No, Grandpa,' she said, 'my mind doesn't work like that. I can never decide anything by thinking, you know, logically thinking, you know, step by step, cause and effect. No, I, myself, I never do anything. It is not I, it is something in me that makes me do things. All that I, myself, can do, for my conscience's sake, is to supply that strange something with all the material data that I can find, and then . . . I wait, and so, you see, I, myself, I don't know a thing, it is that strange something, whatever it is, it can make me invite him, or not invite him, or it can make me forget the whole thing and write a poem instead. So that's that,' she said. 'Anyway,' she added, rising from the bench, 'I promised John we'd go rowing on the Serpentine.'

•

Some twenty minutes later, or a little more perhaps, when crossing the Serpentine Bridge on his way back, he stopped in the middle of the bridge, looked down at the water, and he saw them. Their boat was moving slowly towards him, some ducks and drakes in its wake. The boy pulling and then resting on his oars for a long time, the girl's hand lazily on the tiller. He didn't want them to look up and discover that they had been observed. He sighed, and smiled, and went on. Oh God, how happy they looked! Oh God, please leave them alone. Oh God, please allow them not to have cancer, not to burn alive in an aeroplane, not to end in a madhouse, or a prison, or a poorhouse! This little prayer, which intruded itself into his thoughts so suddenly, of its own volition, took him so much aback that for a moment he was lost in wonder. Was that little prayer forced upon him by the same sort of thing Deborah meant when she said that it wasn't she but something in her that would decide whether to invite John, or not invite him, or forget it all and write a poem instead? Oh God! Oh God! he repeated. This time self-mockingly. Self-mockingly, because was it not he, himself, the little boy Sean D'Eath (as he was called at the time, ages ago) was it not he, himself, who proved experimentally that there is no God. Or, anyhow, no God to speak of. God, who resurrected his own son, but wouldn't resurrect his, Sean's, mother who was killed because some tax-paying women were throwing stones to break somebody's windows. Some God, indeed! And yet, if there is no God, then to say 'Oh God!' has no meaning, and that is surely not true, because he, Sean D'Earth (as he is called now) *knows* that there is a meaning in saying 'Oh God!' And how can there be a meaning in it if the word 'God' points somewhere where there is nothing of the sort, if the word 'God' is just an empty noun, just like the word 'table' would have been an empty noun if there were no tables in the world, or if there were no people, some termites only, for whom a wooden table is not a table but food? But, hold on a moment, now . . . If 'Oh God!' has a meaning and the word 'God' cannot be a noun because, if so, it would be an empty noun (and an empty noun has no meaning) then perhaps God is not a noun at all, perhaps He is a verb! Not something like a 'table' or a 'father', but something like to 'love' or to 'exist'. And if so, then His attributes are not adjectives, like: *good* or *bad* or *omnipotent*, but adverbs, like: *gently now here there ever*, and, if so, if He is a verb, then the greatest theological puzzle of our time would be, Wouldn't it?, whether He is a transitive verb, like *to kill*, or an intransitive verb, like *to die* . . .

He went on walking but he stopped thinking. He had just crossed the Bayswater Road and was no longer among the trees of the Park. Among the trees, he felt safe. The trees didn't care whether he talked to himself, or not. The passers-by did. So it seemed. Thus, trying not to think, so that his lips wouldn't move, he walked briskly towards mournful ever-weeping Paddington.

> What are the golden builders doing
> Near mournful ever-weeping Paddington,
> Standing above that might ruin
> Where Satan the first victory won.

On the corner, opposite Paddington Railway Station, he stopped. He knew there was something he wanted, but what was it? He was searching for the word, but the word seemed to be saying 'I, the word, will show you what I am; I, the word, will tell you how to *say* me, but you must find me first.' Which was a silly thing to say. So he asked the word, 'And *where* can I find you?' And the word answered, 'How can *I* know? It was you who thought you'd find me in Praed Street.'

Praed Street was on his right. So he turned right and marched on. The street was noisy and dirty, and people in Praed Street wouldn't care a damn whether he, Sean D'Earth, was talking to himself or not. They were jostling against each other, going about their own business, in and out of the smelly eating houses, mournful sex shops, photographic shops, the chemist's, the stationer's, the ever-weeping pawnbroker's shop. He looked across the road, and there, of course, was old St Mary's Hospital. Goodness me, St Mary's Hospital! St Mary's Hospital where, more than forty years before, his wife, Prickly Rose, had given birth to his son, Adam, just as the air-raid sirens were wailing and a bomb was dropping near by. That was the day when everybody was so nice to him, the girl serving tea in the canteen, and the young lady in uniform whom, the same evening, he took to the nearby cinema to see *Gone with the Wind* – everybody, except his own Prickly Rose who blamed him for everything, including the timing of the German air raid. And soon after, the young lady in uniform married a Sir Lionel Cooper, who a few years later was killed – they didn't tell her how and why – somewhere in Belgium, of all places – and she also had a child, a boy, called Perceval, who is now a director of a Health Farm or something like that, and is she disappointed with her son Perceval just as he, Sean, is disappointed with his son Adam? (He forgot that he had just received, that very morning, a printed card, edged with black, announcing Lady Cooper's death.) He looked again across the road, at St Mary's Hospital, and saw something he hadn't noticed before: a dark violet-brownish round plaque on the wall:

SIR ALEXANDER FLEMING
1881–1955
DISCOVERED PENICILLIN
IN THE SECOND STOREY
ROOM ABOVE THIS
PLAQUE

Oh well, he looked jealously at the plaque, that's what he used to think his son would be doing, but things are as they are; must they be as they are? Does one need to have lived so long and to have grown so old to understand that things like penicillin, and genetic engineering, and semi-conductors, are *the* things that change the ways of the world, and that the ways of the world are changed by them and not by all those prophets, and stock-exchange puppets, and prime ministers, who believe that it is their own bobbing up and down that rules the waves? Why have you chosen to go that way, Adam? Don't you see, it is the very old damned way, and your hush-hush job will make it only more damnable?

There was a gun shop on the corner. Sporting rifles, over-and-under shotguns, telescopic sights, no, no patriotic old-fashioned dumdum bullets, just ordinary small-shot cartridges and fishing rods. He looked for a hunting horn. There wasn't one. Not in the window, anyway.

He marched on. Eating houses again, and video shops, and Xerox machines, and then, at last, the bookshop. Well, where to find the missing word if not in a bookshop? Or was it a book he wanted? He walked in. Perhaps, when browsing among the books at random, something will jog his memory. He walked from shelf to shelf. Medical books. Physics. Chemistry. Electronics. Art books. Dictionaries. Paperbacks. Blank. Blank. Blank. His memory could not be rushed. He walked out.

There was a small cinema next door to the bookshop. Was

that the cinema he went to . . . with her . . . the day Adam was born . . . to see *Gone with the Wind*? He wasn't sure. The entrance looked so much smaller. And shabbier. But when one is old, everything looks smaller and shabbier. He bought a ticket and walked in. Knowing that it was absurd, he half-expected to see the words 'Gone with the Wind' on the poster displayed by the door, but the title of the film was:

THE WORD PROCESSOR

and the picture on the poster showed a Greek sculpture of a female nude climbing up a Doric column. And yet, as he sat down in the darkness of the back row and looked at the screen, he saw no Greek goddesses. What he saw was a number of ordinary people on the roof garden of a tall office block. It looked like a garden party for the members of the staff. Among them, a young girl. And a man in his forties. There was no music, no dialogue, no sound effects. But there was a running commentary. An impersonal, anonymous VOICE was saying coolly, informatively, what one actually saw happening on the screen. And the spoken words seemed to be more impressive than the pictures they described.

(*the* VOICE *said*)
She sprained her ankle
He comes to her aid
He takes her into the goods lift
He manages a sly feel of one of the two milk-secreting organs on upper front of her body
She pretends not to notice
He lays her on the bench
He presses the button
The lift goes down
He presses the STOP button
The lift stops between floors
He starts to massage the joint connecting her foot with her leg; slender part between this and calf

She lets her other lower limb slide off the bench
He lowers her massaged lower limb down
The terminal part of his left upper limb is rubbing the small
projection in which her female sex mammal mammary
ducts terminate
The terminal part of his right upper limb is undoing his flies
He gets it out in view
She reaches out and feels the stiffness of it
His upper limb goes up her skirt under her knickers and
finds . . .

*Now, all of a sudden, the picture on the screen shows the blue sky
and the green fields and an angelic voice quotes St Matthew:*

The foxes have holes, and the birds of the air have nests; but
the Son of man hath not where to lay his head.

*the blue sky and the green fields fade-out; the interior of the goods
lift fades-in.*

*(the VOICE continues)*

. . . and finds that what-is-both-the-hole-and-the-nest is
running with desire by now
He pulls her knickers down and thrusts his bulging copula-
tory and urinatory organ into her
She grips the sides of the bench and pushes against him
hard
She feels it when he comes off up her
Now they start again but slowly
He removes all her clothes
He kisses the fine filaments growing from skin above her
external genital orifice
He pulls her lower limbs open
She feels his fleshy muscular organ in the mouth, serving
purposes of tasting, licking, swallowing, and of speech

*Suddenly the lift goes down and the next picture is: the office, she
sits at her typewriter/word processor, he approaches*

## D'Eath into D'Earth

*(the* VOICE *continues)*
Next morning
She sits at her word processor
He looks down her mammae
She feels an itch in the place where her lower limbs fork
   from her trunk
She looks at the bulge in his pants

*(now the voice changes to soft* FEMALE VOICE*)*
Such a thing makes her heart flutter in her breast
For when she sees it even for a moment
Then power to speak another word fails her
Instead her tongue freezes into silence
And at once a gentle fire catches through her flesh
And she sees nothing with her eyes
And there's a drumming in her ears
And sweat pours down her
And trembling seizes all of her
And she becomes paler than grass
And she seems to fail almost to the point of death in her
   very self . . .

*And now a* CLOSE-UP *of the* WORD PROCESSOR *appears on the
screen:*

Φαίνεταί μοι κῆνος ἴσος θέοισιν
ἔμμεν' ὤνηρ, ὄττις ἐνάντιός σοι
ἰσδάνει καί πλάσιον ἄδυ φωνεί-
   σας ὐπακούει
καί γελαίσας ἰμέροεν, τό μ' ἦ μάν
καρδίαν ἐν στήθεσιν ἐπτόαισεν,
ὠς γάρ ἔς σ' ἴδω βρόχε', ὤς με φώναι-
   σ' οὐδ' ἔν ἔτ' εἴκει,
ἀλλ' ἄκαν μεν γλώσσα πέπαγε, λέπτον
δ' αὔτικα χρῶι πῦρ ὐπαδεδρόμηκεν,
ὀππάτεσσι δ' οὐδ' ἔν ὄρημμ', ἐπιρρόμ-
   βεισι δ' ἄκουαι,
κάδ δέ μ' ἴδρως κάκχέεται, τρόμος δέ
παῖσαν ἄγρει, χλωροτέρα δέ ποίας
ἔμμι, τεθνάκην δ' ὀλίγω 'πιδεύης
   φαίνομ' ἔμ' αὔται.

67

From the neighbouring darkness on his right, a timid female voice asked:

'What's that? Is it Arabic?'

'No,' he said. 'It's Greek.'

'Why Greek?' the timid voice said. 'The girl isn't Greek. She looks English.'

'It's a Greek love poem. Ancient. By a girl called Sappho. She was Lesbian. Born in Lesbos.'

'But the girl in the film is not a Lesbian, is she?' the timid voice said and a timid hand slightly touched his.

'No,' he said. 'But that's one of those *non sequiturs* . . .'

'What's that?' the timid voice asked.

'Oh, that's Latin.'

He didn't explain further, for the WORD PROCESSOR ended and the screen lightened with the title of the next short film: MANE TICKLE FARES. He was never to learn what the word 'tickle' was meant to convey, because just now a black man in a black tailcoat decorated with medals appeared on the screen between two white nudes, and the blackness of the black man's face jogged his memory . . . *Bukumla!* of course. 'Bukumla' was the word he was searching for, 'Bukumla,' he repeated and got up, and the timid voice in the darkness on his right said, 'Oh, don't go!', and the hand grasped his hand for a second, and he felt the warmth of the hand, but he was afraid he might again forget the word 'Bukumla', and, as the two white Furies on the silver screen started tearing the black man's clothes off his rippling muscles, he turned away from the voice in the darkness and marched on to the word EXIT, shining above the door by the screen.

The exit door opened into a narrow street at the back of the cinema. Repeating the word 'Bukumla', he turned left and walked to the corner of Edgware Road, and then left again, *Bukumla Bukumla*, to the corner of Praed Street, and left again, *Bukumla Bukumla*, past the entrance to the cinema – and to the bookshop. But the bookshop was closed by now. He stood in front of it, feeling old and silly, when, suddenly, in the semidarkness of the bookshop window, he saw it! A thick volume:

> ECOLOGY & BIOGEOGRAPHY
> IN
> BUKUMLA

In Bukumla, there was a revolution. Wherever there is a revolution, there is some looting. Were he in Bukumla, and were he strong enough, he could break the plate-glass windowpane and take the book. On the other hand, were he in Bukumla, he wouldn't need it. That was the silly logic of reality. So he marched on.

There was a little pub, a nice little pub on the corner. He walked in and asked for Bukumla bullets. When the barman said, 'I beg your pardon, sir?' he said, 'I'm sorry, I meant gin and tonic.' And again he felt old and silly. Why had he ordered a gin and tonic if what he wanted was whisky and soda? He took his gin and tonic to a little table by the window. There was something *non sequitur* in all that. Or was it only that he had forgotten something? When the antecedent has erased itself in your memory, is your affirmation of the consequent a *non sequitur*? Of course, not. Of course, yes. Of course, yes and no. Everything in this world is *yes and no*. On the other hand, everything is linked together and nothing is *non sequitur*. He felt old and tired. He looked through the window, it was dark already, it was raining, and the little water drops he saw falling on the windowpane seemed to sound in his ears like the Sapphic stanza, translated again into the Morse code of his boy scout's childhood:

> dadi dadi dadidi dadi dadi
> dadi dadi dadidi dadi dadi

69

dadi dadi dadidi dadi dadi
dadidi dadi

No, the girl in that film was not Deborah, definitely not. But
the loudspeaker voice reciting Sappho could have been hers.
Oh, it doesn't matter. Why should it? Why should marble
nudes be all right, but those photographed – vulgar? Why
should matter-of-fact descriptions be obscene, and Greek lyrics
– beautiful? And what was that word processor meant to
show? Was it meant to be funny, or was it meant to show
some deeper meaning?

For ten long minutes he stared into the distance, beyond
the walls of the pub. Then he looked at his watch. That was
the day of the week his son came to visit him. At 8 p.m.
punctually. Which meant five minutes past eight. Because
even his unpunctuality was punctual.

## THREE

## Picture Postcard from Bukumla

'Carissima,' Dr Goldfinger said, browsing among books in that *librairie* of the Rive Gauche, 'I've found something we have never heard of. By your beloved Anatole France.'

'Really?' Princess Zuppa said.

But Madame B., the *libraire*, butted in: 'Anatole France was a great man and a great humanist. His *L'Île des Pingouins*, for example, is infinitely more subtle and more human than that vulgarity of your English policeman who called himself Orwell. But, I beg your pardon, you are not English of course, you are Italian, *n'est ce pas?*'

They (Princess Zuppa and Dr Goldfinger) used to visit Paris at least once a year, but they knew it much better as it was long ago, before they were born. *Fin de Siècle. La Belle Époque* . . . Their knowledge of the period was extensive and peculiar. They could tell where in the boulevard St Michel was the brasserie Steinbach in which the members of *Philosopharium* gathered twice a week in 1910 or 1911; or, for example, that it was outside the *Closerie des Lilas*, on the terrace, that there took place the historical encounter of Cardinal Pölätüo and Charles Maurras, discussing how to get rid of Guillaume Apollinaire (the Cardinal's presumptive bastard son); or, to take a later instance, that it wasn't in *Le Dôme, La Rotonde*, or *La Coupole* but in *Le Select* (much less expensive) that Ilia Ehrenburg conceived his *Julio Jurenito* in the early twenties.

'It's called *Sur la Voie Glorieuse*,' Dr Goldfinger continued, brandishing the book. 'Ha, ha, listen! It starts with a eulogy of Le Roi Albert, who joined the army as a simple soldier.

*"Roi, les républicains saluent en vous un héros et un juste."* ' He turned the pages. 'Now, listen, DEBOUT POUR LA DERNIÈRE GUERRE! Ha ha! How funny! He seriously thought the 1914–1918 would be the last war! Incredible! He quotes H. G. Wells. Says Wells's prophecies have become true, only it's not the Martians but the German professors who have made the war to be *métallurgique et chimique* . . . after which they will make it *bactériologique et, après la lutte des gaz délétères et des liquides enflammés, ils inaugureront la lutte des tubes de culture . . ."* '

He stopped. They were not listening. Princess Zuppa was looking at a picture postcard pinned to the panelling by Madame B.'s desk, while Madame B. was staring at Princess Zuppa. *'Pardonnez-moi,* Madame,' Princess Zuppa said, 'but this postcard . . . The picture reminds me of a place in Bukumla . . .'

'It *is* Bukumla,' Madame B. said.

'Really?' Princess Zuppa asked.

*'Si,'* Madame B. said.

'How extraordinary,' Princess Zuppa said.

'Not at all,' Madame B. said.

'No?' Princess Zuppa asked.

'No,' Madame B. said. 'It's a postcard from my nephew who is there now.'

'In Bukumla?' Princess Zuppa asked.

'Not exactly *in* Bukumla. Just across the border. On the sea. If one can talk about borders in a jungle.'

'I hope he's safe there,' Princess Zuppa said.

'Oh yes, of course he is safe. In 1968 he was a young revolutionary, as an *étudiant,* schoolboy actually. But now he is a grown man, selling *ordinateurs* to black illiterates.'

'I said I hoped he was safe, Madame, because there is a revolution in Bukumla,' Princess Zuppa said.

'Indeed,' Madame B. said.

72

'. . . and the newspapers say the President of Bukumla was abducted. And killed. Hanged,' Princess Zuppa insisted.

'Yes, that's what they say, *les journaux*,' Madame B. said after a short pause.

'You think, Madame, that he might not have been killed?' Princess Zuppa asked.

But for Madame B. that was the end of the conversation on the subject. She turned to Dr Goldfinger, took *Sur la Voie Glorieuse* by Anatole France from his hands, and asked, 'Do you wish me to put it aside for you?'

'By all means, yes, please, do, *chère* Madame, I'll love to have it,' Dr Goldfinger said.

'Do you think, Madame, that he might still be alive?' Princess Zuppa asked again.

'Who?' Madame B. asked.

'The President of Bukumla.'

'Oh,' said Madame B., 'that's what the papers do not say.'

Dr Goldfinger gave Princess Zuppa a wink and, turning to Madame B., exclaimed, '*Mon Dieu!* It's one o'clock! I'm as hungry as a wolf. *C'est l'heure de déjeuner.* There must be a restaurant somewhere near, chère Madame, mustn't there, one of those restaurants for the *gourmet,* where *on mange de bonne cuisine,* I mean the real *cuisine bourgeoise, la cuisine française* . . . There is? Five minutes' walk? How marvellous! I hope *que vous nous ferez le plaisir d'accepter de déjeuner avec nous,* surely it will be possible for you, chère Madame, to write a little note saying "*Reviens dans 2 heures*" or, better still, "*2 heures et demi*" and come with us, you will? *Grazie, molto gentile!* Excellent. We shall talk literature. *La Belle Époque.* French novels, French cooking, French wines. What more can a man want?'

•

They were given a table in the *entresol*. La patronne herself came to discuss with Madame B., one after another, all the items on the à la carte menu. They didn't discuss wine. Only foreigners discuss wine.

'At the time of Louis the Fourteenth,' Madame B. said, '*les gens de lettres* were drunkards. At the time of Brillat-Savarin they became gluttons, which – as he said – was an improvement. At the end of your beloved *Belle Époque* they starved and drank absinthe. And now?'

'They drink Coca Cola and eat hamburgers,' Dr Goldfinger said.

'Alas, even in Paris,' Madame B. said. And, after a moment of munching, she added, 'I think I could find for you one of the first editions of *Physiologie du Goût*. Or, is it only *La Belle Époque* period that you are interested in?'

'Chère Madame,' Dr Goldfinger said, 'I'm afraid I'm not a collector. And Principessa and I, we are so interested in your *Belle Époque* only because, for us, it is like a fairy-tale. So far from the reality of life . . .'

Madame B. put down her fork and knife.

'Did I hear you saying "Principessa"?' she asked.

'Yes, Madame, you did,' Dr Goldfinger said. 'And what I'm just longing to tell you, Madame, is why Principessa is so much interested in that deposed President of Bukumla . . .'

'I am a republican,' Madame B. said. 'Which means there is nobody above me. Nor below me. But I do like titles. Liking aristocratic titles is like liking limited editions: *10 ex. sur papier de Chine numérotés 1 à 10. 30 ex. sur papier du Japon numérotés 11 à 40. 125 ex. sur papier de Hollande numérotés 41 à 165.* It is like liking the old well-bound books, olive leather, gilt-tooled with scrollwork, etc., gilt top edge, front and bottom edges uncut. I love them. I buy them and sell them. But what I read last thing in the evening and first thing in the morning, in bed, is paperbacks.'

'Good,' Princess Zuppa said.

'Let me tell you, Madame, why Princess Zuppa is so interested in what has happened in Bukumla,' Dr Goldfinger said.

### Picture Postcard from Bukumla

'*Et voilà, il revient à ses moutons,*' Madame B. said.

'Why are you so reluctant to talk about Bukumla?' he insisted.

'Are you from a newspaper?' Madame B. asked.

'*Mais non*, chère Madame,' he said. 'Nothing to do with the press. Nothing to do with politics. Nothing to do with the police. What I'm trying to tell you is that Princess Zuppa is very personally interested in what has happened in Bukumla, and especially in what has happened to the President of Bukumla, and that is because she is his sister.'

'*Mais comment?*' Madame B. exclaimed. 'How come? How can that be? He's black, isn't he?'

'So you think that he's still alive?'

'I didn't say that, did I?'

'You said he *is* black, not he was black.'

'Well, black people don't change their colour when they die, do they? Dead or alive, he's still black, isn't he?'

'He is black because his mother is black,' Dr Goldfinger said. 'But his father was white. His father was a Polish general; during the last war he found himself first in Bukumla, and then in Italy . . . So you see . . . That's how it happened that Princess Zuppa is the President's half-sister.'

All of a sudden in a pensive mood, Madame B. took a sip of coffee and a sip of liqueur and said in a melancholy tone of voice, 'In Majorca, some years ago, I met a nice English lady who had a child fathered by a Polish general. Was that how those generals were fighting the war? Producing bastards all over the world?'

She didn't realize what she had just said. Or perhaps she did and that's why she very rapidly now said, 'All right, I'll tell you all I know. It was my nephew. My nephew and his colleagues. There in the jungle. They came across the President at the very moment he was going to be hanged. So they rescued him. And took him with them. But some shots were fired and they didn't want to be involved. They were dealing

75

with computers and not with some local politics. So they sold him for seventy-eight bottles of whisky to an English skipper who took him aboard and put out to sea at once.'

'Where to?'

'I don't know.'

'What was the name of the boat?'

'Oh yes. The name of the boat. Most unsuitable, I should say. The name of the boat was *The Resurrection*.'

Back in the hotel, they telephoned Rome. Palazzo d'Ormespant. Jonathan the Third answered. Which was fine. They wouldn't, of course, dream of asking to talk to the Cardinal. His Eminence was too old and too slow for that kind of activity. He was so old by now that most people, including those in the Vatican, had forgotten about his existence. Those who remembered thought he would live for ever. That legend was fortified by the prophecy inspired by one of his biographers who dared speculate that in 2022, when the Cardinal would be 200 years old, the Post Office Express Delivery Services will be using a device that scans and destroys one by one all the molecules of the three-dimensional object in the mailbag and sending the information to another device, far away, which will recreate it from identical but not the same molecules. That's how our Cardinal is dispatched to the New Vatican (USA) for the election of the new Pontiff. As it happens, His Eminence, disintegrated in Rome, is received and integrated (due to some human error) not by one station in New York but by twelve stations in different parts of America, from which, subsequently, twelve identical cardinals make their way to the New Vatican, thus embarrassing the theologians by making them face the following problems: How many souls have they? How many votes have they? How will the newly acquired characteristics start to differentiate them? How to deal with the new possibilities of asexual reproduction, immorality, immortality? Original Sin?

## Picture Postcard from Bukumla

'Dear Jonathan,' Princess Zuppa said into the telephone mouthpiece, 'no, no, don't disturb His Eminence. It is you, Jonathan, I want. There is something *you* could do for us, you see?'

He liked Princess Zuppa, and said, 'For you, Your Serene Highness, everything!'

'Well,' she said, 'I'd better ask Dr Goldfinger to explain.'

Jonathan respected Dr Goldfinger who, once upon a time, during the stewardship of one of the other two Jonathans, saved Pölätüo's life when the Archbishop of Merangue inadvertently pronounced the name of Guillaume Apollinaire, upon which a fishbone stuck in the Cardinal's throat.

'Yes?' said Jonathan.

'I shall put it in a nutshell,' Dr Goldfinger said. 'There is a boat bobbing about somewhere on the waters of the Atlantic. All we know about her is that she's bigger than a dinghy and smaller than a liner. We also know that she is English. Can you find her? Using your international, universal connections, can you find her position and destination?'

'You haven't told me her name, *Dottore*,' Jonathan said.

'I was afraid you'd ask,' Dr Goldfinger said. 'Well, brace yourself, Jonathan. Her name is *The Resurrection*.'

There was a deep silence between Paris and Rome. After which Jonathan the Third asked, 'Have I got you right, *Dottore*? There is an English boat somewhere in the Atlantic. She is bigger than a dinghy and smaller than a liner. Her name is *The Resurrection*, and you wish me to find her position and destination.'

'That is correct,' Dr Goldfinger said.

Pause.

'Now, Dr Goldfinger, please tell me straight: is this meant to be a parable or is it on the level?'

'It is on the level, Jonathan.'

Though the Cardinal himself was half-forgotten, the influential machinery of Palazzo d'Ormespant still existed and was

77

kept in working order, first by Jonathan the First, then by Jonathan the Second, and now by Jonathan the Third, who was very well aware of the fact that its power did not emanate from him personally.

Five hours after his conversation with Princess Zuppa and Dr Goldfinger, he phoned them back. 'Having referred your problem to His Eminence,' he said, 'having obtained his *placet* and *exequatur*, I have made some necessary inquiries, the result of which is as follows:

'Tomorrow, you will go to Fouquet's Bar in Les Champs-Élysées, to be there at noon, exactly. You'll find a table on the terrace and you'll order two coffees, which will cost you 34.50 francs for two, *service compris*. You must take a book with you, no matter what book, but one of you will be reading it by holding it upside down. That's all you have to do. So far. There will be there a person who'll be observing you. If the person doesn't like you, the person will go, and that will be the end of the story. But if the person approves of you, the person will come to your table, holding a newspaper with a crossword puzzle. And the person will ask you, "Could you help me, Madame et Monsieur, *bigger than a dinghy and smaller than a liner*, twelve letters." To which you will answer, "*Resurrection*." That's all I can tell you. The rest is up to you. His Eminence sends to both of you his blessings. *Addio!*'

•

The Champs-Élysées, between the Rond Point and the Arc de Triomphe, were crammed with people. Between their legs, in front of Fouquet's Bar, a dark-skinned woman was sitting on the pavement, at the carriageway edge of it, a sleeping baby on her lap. The baby was big, must have been some nine years of age, or ten. At the moment Dr Goldfinger was giving her money, three men appeared. They didn't bully the woman. They let her grasp Dr Goldfinger's coins before chasing her off the pavement.

The man in the middle must have been armed. He didn't even bother to disguise the enormous bullet-proof jacket, reaching down to his knees, which made him look as if he were inside a big cardboard box, loosely draped by his *imperméable*. The man on his left and the man on his right were surely past retirement age; one could have been a pawn-shop clerk, the other a soup-kitchen cashier, recalled to duty for this special occasion. But what was the occasion? They didn't know. A visit? Of the king of Spain? Or Mrs Thatcher? Or Mr Gorbachev? Lucky 3½-lingual Helvetia. No such fuss would have been made for their president, whose burden of rule never goes beyond the 31st of December.

The three men marched off. For Princess Zuppa and Dr Goldfinger, that was, that day, their hors d'œuvre encounter with French plain-clothes policemen. The entrée was to follow.

They found a little table on the terrace and ordered coffee. 'We must behave, the "person" is observing us,' Princess Zuppa said. But which one was *the* person, they didn't even try to guess. There must have been some fifty?, sixty?, eighty?, perhaps a hundred people sitting at the small tables and talking and talking and talking. They were all different, and yet, not counting a few tourists, they all looked as if they had something special in common. 'Well,' Princess Zuppa said, 'I know what they have in common. What they have in common is the very fact that they are here, now, at this time of the working day. They must all be free-lance. This is where they are working. They are people who need to see other people and need to be seen in the act of seeing them. Professionally.'

Dr Goldfinger jumped up.

'Where is the book?' he asked.

'You were sitting on it,' Princess Zuppa said.

It was *Sur la Voie Glorieuse* that he had bought the day before at Mme B.'s. He opened it now, and turned it upside down.

'Can you read upside down?' Princess Zuppa asked.

'Of course I can,' he said. And started: ' ' ".dial port tse li :erviv tuep en iuq ertsnom nu tnof ne slI .erreug al tneut sli ;xiap al éut tneiava slI .naimuh'd erocne tiatser iul iuq ec tuot semra sed tra'l à étô tno sdnamellA seL" '

They laughed. They laughed and didn't notice where the young smiling man had come from. But there he was, standing by their table, smiling. Everything about him was smiling. He had smilingly tousled hair, smiling eyes, a smiling voice, a smiling T-shirt, and smiling rings on his fingers. *'Excusez-moi, Madame, excusez-moi, Monsieur,'* he said, smiling, 'but I feel you can help me with my crossword puzzle. Here it is: *Bigger than a dinghy, smaller than a liner*, twelve letters.'

Dr Goldfinger was lost for words, for a moment, but Princess Zuppa said at once: *'Resurrection.'* Upon which the young man conjured another chair from somewhere and sat down at their table.

'Pierrot,' said the young man.

'Zuppa,' said Princess Zuppa.

'Arturo,' said Dr Goldfinger.

They shook hands.

'Enchanté, Madame Zuppa, Enchanté, Monsieur Arturo,' the smiling young man said. 'How do you like Paris?'

'I love it,' Princess Zuppa said.

'And so do I,' Dr Goldfinger said.

'Good!' the smiling young man called Pierrot said. He took a sip of the *jus de fruit* he had brought with him. *'Eh bien,'* he said. 'My orders are to help you, and your business is not something I'm going to pry into. But there are one or two things I should know. What are you actually interested in? *The Resurrection* herself? Her crew? Or her cargo?'

'Her cargo,' Princess Zuppa said.

'That's bad. Considering what her cargo is.'

'I mean her human cargo,' Princess Zuppa said.

'How many?' Pierrot asked.

'How many what?'

'How many souls?'

'Just one eternal soul in just one, I hope still living, black body.'

'Do you wish just to learn about it, or do you want to see it?'

'Preferably the latter,' Princess Zuppa said.

'No violence is intended? Or expected?'

'Absolutely no violence.'

'Good. Well . . . Her human cargo might already have been disembarked at her first port of call, so to speak.'

'Which is where?' Princess Zuppa asked.

'You mean: Where does *The Resurrection* leave her human cargo, Madame?' he said and it seemed that one could *hear* his smile. '*Eh bien*, I'm afraid the name will not tell you much.' Now his eyes lightened and his voice became quite lyrical, as he said: 'If you draw a perhaps a little wobbly line going due west from Land's End, Cornwall, and another line going south from County Cork, in the Republic of Ireland, it is not unlikely that the two lines will cross exactly at the point where a big mountain grows from the bottom of the sea so high upwards that its green head sticks permanently above sea level, even during the highest of tides. Still, it is too small to be found on our ordinary maps, and even the Admiralty charts mark it only as a "danger rock" which, of course, it is not. It is a little island. Called *Hobson's Island*. And I can take you there.'

'Great!' Princess Zuppa said.

'Yes, it could be fun,' Pierrot said. 'But,' he added, 'before you decide, I think you must be told what's involved . . .'

'Money doesn't count,' she said.

'It isn't a question of money,' he said. 'It's politics. Geopolitics.' He took a paper napkin and drew on it three dots. 'This one,' he said, 'is our Hobson's Island. As you see, it's situated more or less at the same distance from the coast of Ireland as from the coast of the UK. Which fact is of some import. Because it has never been said anywhere to whom it belongs. Politically. To Great Britain or to the Republic of Ireland. Both governments prefer to keep quiet about it. As if they were afraid that if they say, "It's mine", the other will say, "No, it's mine", and an unholy row, which nobody wants, will follow. They are satisfied with the *status quo*. So is our, the French, government. We don't want to see any changes there. But we would like to know what's going on. Because something seems to be going on there and we don't know what.' He drew another dot on the paper napkin. 'Now, this dot is Brest,' he said. 'If we go from here north-west we also hit Hobson's Island. But if we go there officially, the British may think we are going to claim it for France, and they may lose their nerve and declare that it is and has always been British, which will make the Irish say it is Irish, and somebody may need some military glory for the sake of an electoral victory, and things may happen that nobody wants to happen, and so it has been decided that I will sail there as an amateur sailor, no uniform, no arms, no cloak and dagger, no camera even, just a Geiger counter and a good eye. And that's how things were when you appeared out of the blue. At a most opportune moment. Just think. An Italian couple. Rich and eccentric. Nothing to do with politics. Pay me a colossal sum of money to take them to see the tiniest island on this side of the Atlantic!'

'How much?' Princess Zuppa asked.

He smiled again.

'We give you a receipt, but you don't pay us a *sou*. You'll have the receipt so that you can show it if somebody is suspicious.'

'With respect, Pierrot, doesn't all that sound like helping you to spy?' Dr Goldfinger said.

Pierrot's smile burst into bubbling laughter.

'Oh darling,' Princess Zuppa said. 'It's not like you to make linguistic difficulties. To explore an island that nobody wants to have if nobody else has it – is not spying!'

82

'I liked the way you said "with respect", Arturo,' Pierrot
said. 'Spying is an empirical search for Truth,' he added,
but his thoughts were somewhere else. She looks young, he
thought, but she must be over forty, mustn't she? And he,
Arturo, must be some twenty years older. Now, how to accom-
modate them on the boat? He lifted his hand and waved it.
But not for the waiter. A young girl in jeans, who was sitting
alone not far away, got up and came to their table. 'Let me
introduce you,' Pierrot said. 'Marie-Claire, Madame Zuppa.'

'Enchantée, Madame,' Marie-Claire said.

'Marie-Claire, Monsieur Arturo,' Pierrot said.

'Enchantée, Monsieur,' Marie-Claire said.

'Marie-Claire is my crew, and she's also my wife,' Pierrot
said. 'Or should I have said she's my wife and she's also my
crew? We shall be sailing together.'

'Great,' Princess Zuppa said.

'*Et voilà* . . . ' Pierrot said. 'We would start from a little place
near Brest. It's a small sailing boat but with a rather powerful
cruising-speed motor. Two cabins. Two berths each. Madame
Zuppa can share a cabin with Marie-Claire, if she wishes.'

'That will not be necessary,' Princess Zuppa said. 'When do
we start? I look forward to it! I'm sure you do too, Arturo.'

'*Ubi tu Zuppa, ibi ego Arturo,*' said Arturo Goldfinger.

## FOUR

## The English Family Shepherd

There is no mystery in what we know about Hobson's Island.
No mystery, only just a number of questions to which it is not
easy to find a documented answer. One knows that in 1923
(or was it 1924?) the whole island, uninhabited, never culti-
vated, was bought by an American multi-millionaire, called
Thomas Hobson. *Question one*: Whom did he buy it from?
There is no record of the deal either in London or in Dublin.
The place where some documentation must have been
deposited is Switzerland. But the Swiss don't give away their
secrets and don't gossip. *Question two*: Did Mr Hobson buy
the island because it was called Hobson's Island, or is it called
Hobson's Island because it was he who bought it?

The name HOBSON'S ISLAND does not appear in any gazet-
teers before 1923. The only item you can find under HOBSON
in ordinary dictionaries or in the indexes of some learned
books is HOBSON'S CHOICE, which takes us back to a Thomas
Hobson (1544?–1631) who produced the early seventeenth-
century equivalent of Henry Ford's apocryphal dictum: 'You
can have your car of any colour, so long as it is black.' With
Mr Thomas Hobson, a Cambridge livery-stable keeper, it was:
'You can hire any horse, so long as you choose the one that
stands nearest the stable door.' Did the American Thomas
Hobson believe, or like to believe, that the other Thomas
Hobson, the liveryman, was one of his ancestors? Did he come
to the old country, like so many Americans, in search of (or
to put down) roots? But, if so, why didn't he buy some property in Cambridgeshire (his alleged ancestor's country), why

did he choose that little speck of earth surrounded by the sea, so far away from everywhere? What did he want to do with it?

These, and all further '*Questions*' overlap, so there's no point in numbering them any more. The unquestionable fact remains that, as soon as he bought the Island, he brought some builders from Ireland, engineers from England, architects from the USA, materials from all over the world, and started to build an enormous house. For what sort of a purpose? – that's another unanswerable and unnumbered question. A hotel? No, a hotel of that size would have to have a big kitchen and a big laundry, and there was nothing of the sort in the house. A private mammoth mansion-house for himself? The disposition of so many rooms of various shapes and sizes suggested that it couldn't possibly have been built for that purpose. And the configuration of the enormous hall would make it most unsuitable for theatrical or musical activities. Neither could it have been an architect's folly – there was nothing unusual about its form or colour or building materials. It seemed that the only Don-Quixotery in the landscape was provided by the windmills (still in good working order). Two windmills pumped water from artesian wells to tanks on the roof, two others produced electricity. But what was the whole building meant to be for? Perhaps Mr and Mrs Shepherd (of whom more in a moment), perhaps they knew. But they are dead. And their successors (Mr and Mrs Shepherd junior) never asked, never were told, and didn't know.

It was an advertisement in the *Farmer*, Christmas 1925, ('*animal-loving, vegetarian couple, assured livelihood, as caretakers in an isolated place*') that brought the original Shepherds to the Island. Thomas Hobson (whom they called 'The Governor') took to them right away. And so did they to him. They liked the spacious farmhouse specially built for them near the Big House. The only thing they didn't like, and were puzzled by, was that he didn't want them to have any animals. Finally and reluctantly, after long deliberations, he consented to their having a cow. For the sake of milk. He wanted them to be caretakers, not farmers, he said. They may have an orchard and a kitchen garden as big as they wish, but no animals – well, all right – other than a cow. Once a month, a boat – from Ireland and, in rotation, from Cornwall – would bring them whatever they ordered, within reason. Including things like books, sausages, and bacon. Still, why 'animal-loving, vegetarian couple', who were allowed to buy and bring sausages and bacon from across the water, were not allowed to keep animals, that was another of those questions which one had to stop numbering. Was it that 'The Governor' didn't want animals to be killed on the Island? Perhaps. But this was just a conjecture.

They settled down happily in 1926. And when they said, 'Goodbye, Governor. Happy crossing, sir,' as Thomas Hobson was embarking his yacht for the return voyage to America, they didn't know they were not to see him again, nor did they know that they would be left alone on the Island for many years, till – to keep them company – their son Gregory was born, and two years later a daughter Georgina.

His (Thomas Hobson's) millions, which were multiplying exponentially, like rabbits, during the reign, first of Warren Gamaliel Harding, riddled with corruption (1921–3), and then that of Calvin Coolidge's low taxation and *laissez-faire* policy (1923–9), vanished all of a sudden with the 1929 Wall Street Crash that started the Great Wailing Depression. Having lost his millions, but not his various commitments, and not being able to solve the national financial problems, he decided to solve his own personal problem by self-defenestration, i.e. by jumping out of a thirty-second-floor window.

At that time he was a widower, had no brothers, no sisters, but he had a son. A teenager called Thomas Gamaliel Hobson, T.G.H. for short. It was the lawyers who took care of T.G.H.'s education *in loco parentis*. The lawyers knew about Hobson's

Island, and they were puzzled to see that it was not mentioned in the Hobson assets. They made some inquiries and found out that the Island seemed not to be Hobson's property, it seemed to belong to a mysterious trust, administered by some bankers in Switzerland, who proved to be uncommunicative, not to say cagey about it. As the lawyers, anyway, wouldn't have liked the idea of making the value of the Island available to meet debts, they were not in a hurry to pursue the matter. And so months and then years rolled by, and then came September 1939, and the Second Great War in Europe. T.G.H. was already in his late twenties. But the USA remained neutral for the first years of the war (as it was for the first years of the First Great War) and it was only after the Japanese attack on Pearl Harbor (December 1941) that President Roosevelt declared war on the Axis.

And so, it was in 1942 that T.G.H. (First-Lieutenant USAF) found himself in England where, soon after, he met Mrs Sean D'Earth, otherwise called (even by her husband) 'Prickly Rose', who had just given birth to a little boy they named Adam, and became more and more prickly to everybody, except to T.G.H., whom she soon managed to convince that he was not really a homosexual, and with whom – after the end of the war – she absconded to America.

If what Sean D'Earth told his son Adam was true, if he never divorced Prickly Rose, then her subsequent marriage to T.G.H. in Reno was bigamous, which fact, so long as nobody (except God) knows about it, doesn't affect anybody, not even the child which she, at her advanced age, gave birth to in America, a little boy whom they decided to call Thomas Lancelot Hobson, T.L.H. for short.

As for the Shepherds and their Island, the war didn't affect them; anyway, it didn't affect them terribly. Just before it started (actually it was the very day Mrs Shepherd told Mr Shepherd she was quite sure she was pregnant), a boat came from England with a dozen uniformed men bringing some short-wave wireless sets and some other electronic equipment, and installed the lot under the roof of the Big House. They told the Shepherds that they (the Shepherds) would be paid one pound a week and would be responsible for the safety of the apparatus left in their charge, upon which they (the uniformed men) departed and never appeared again. However, the one pound a week was regularly paid to the Shepherd's deposit account in a bank in Cornwall and, the order to pay never having been countermanded, it went on being paid for forty years and henceforth, which – with the interest added every six months – produced the sum of . . . (take your electronic calculator and calculate it for yourself) thus contributing to the devaluation of the English currency.

Their usual allowance (or fee, or salary, or whatever else they called it) continued to be sent regularly from neutral Switzerland to their current account in a bank in neutral Ireland. Nor had the war stopped the regular visits (or, rather, 'visitations' by a Swiss gentleman-banker called Herr Schmied who used to come every two or three years via France or England, and – during the war – via Ireland, though he was soon replaced by another Swiss gentleman-banker, called Herr Fischer.

Living alone on the Island, not used to seeing human faces except their own, and – now and again – those of an Irish fisherman bringing them some tinned food, salt, sugar, condensed milk, and of a Cornish fisherman bringing a pair of new trousers for Mr Shepherd, and a brassière for the Missus (he, himself, would rarely, and only in very calm weather, venture to use his little boat with an outboard engine) – they obviously felt not at their ease when a stranger came to inspect how they were doing, especially, for them, such an exceptionally strange stranger as Herr Schmied, or Herr Fischer. 'Do you find everything all right, sir?' they would ask, anxiously and shyly. 'Yes, it is,' Herr Schmied and then (when Herr Schmied retired) Herr Fischer would answer in a matter-of-fact way. 'Is there anything we have neglected to do?' they would ask. 'No, everything is fine,' Herr Schmied and then Herr Fischer would answer. What they really wanted to ask, and didn't dare, was not so much what they should not do as whether there was anything they would be allowed to do and were not doing because they didn't know that they would. Especially something about the cow. Their main worry was the cow.

When the late Mr Thomas Hobson, who didn't want them to keep animals on the Island, consented to their having just one milking cow, neither he nor they thought about it that a milking cow is not a *perpetuum mobile* machine that would go on and on producing milk; they just didn't think about it that the milking season doesn't go on for ever. To produce milk, a cow needs to give birth to a calf, and to be able to calve, she needs a rendezvous with a bull, which fact meant that they would have to have *three* animals on the island. They thought of artificial insemination, but that would still mean *two* animals: the cow and the calf. And so, when their cow dried off, they ordered condensed milk to be added to their delivery list. They could, of course, have sent the 'dried-off' cow back and brought another milking mother to the Island. Actually, they had already done that twice, and so the present cow, Matilda, was their third one. But it's not so easy, and too costly, to transport big animals across the sea, such passage being more expensive than their meat value, and, on the other hand, a cow is the sort of creature one becomes friendly with, and especially when she is the only companion on an island. And so they kept her in her 'dried-off' state, and then in her barren state, for many years, often asking themselves: when she dies her natural death, would they be allowed to have a goat instead, goat's milk being still more nourishing, and a goat's size and weight much easier to transport across the sea. Still, they were shy to ask Herr Schmied, and then Herr Fischer, such a question. They just didn't know how their

Swiss minds worked. What if they said: 'If that's what troubles you, we don't need you. Go away!' Well, where could they go? To England? They had just heard Mr Neville Chamberlain saying on the Radio (27 September 1938): *'How horrible , fantastic, incredible, it is that we should be digging trenches and trying on gas masks here because of a quarrel in a faraway country between people of whom we know nothing.'*

Well, Mr Shepherd didn't like the idea of digging trenches and trying on gas masks, and – who knows? – being conscripted, maybe. And so, where else could they go? To Ireland? With all those Catholics, among whom they would feel more isolated than they were on their Hobson's Island? No, oh no. No, especially as Mrs Shepherd was now quite sure that she was pregnant. Herr Schmied might object to their having another animal on the Island, but, surely, he couldn't object to their having a baby, could he?

She gave birth naturally and with great ease. Thanks, perhaps, to her plain living and her gorgeous, magnificent pelvis. Her breasts were full of milk which, when she pressed them, spurted out in two perfect white parabolas. As there was no priest, no registry office on the Island, Mr Shepherd went to the Big House where there was a big library room, found a Bible, took it to his farmhouse (that was the first time he had taken anything from the Big House to the farmhouse) and on the flyleaf he wrote in indelible pencil:

*Today July 1939* [he wasn't sure which day of the month and day of the week it was] *my wife Mrs Shepherd gave birth to a baby boy of the male sex whom we shall call Gregory.*

> *In witness of the event:*
> *I Mr Shepherd himself.*

Soon (was it already the beginning of September?) the wireless set started to play 'God save the King' (George VI), and they learned that the war had started. All the same, the orchard produced apples and pears as in peacetime, the garden – cabbages and lettuce and green peas and potatoes and tomatoes; the shelves in the larder were packed with paper bags of flour and sugar and salt and margarine and condensed milk; the sewing machine was busy and so were the knitting needles and crochet hooks and scissors cutting Irish linen into various patterns. All over the world old men were sending young men to kill, while on Hobson's Island the spring blossomed into summer, the summer matured into autumn, the autumn nodded into winter, and yet nobody came to make use of the electronic gadgets abandoned under the roof of the Big House.

The warmth of the Gulf Stream, flowing from the faraway Gulf of Mexico, tempered the Island's winter with the green softness swelling slowly into the new spring. Little Gregory was learning to walk, then little Gregory was learning to talk, then Mrs Shepherd became pregnant again, and the next summer a new screaming face appeared from between her hips to keep them company on the Island. The event took place the same day Matilda, the cow, died the natural death of old age. Both facts were duly registered by Mr Shepherd on the flyleaf of the Bible: the death of Matilda, the cow, and the birth of the little baby girl they decided to call Georgina. There occurred, the same day, still another event which, subsequently, had to be 'duly registered' on the flyleaf of the Bible.

It started with an empty bottle which the incoming tide washed up. The bottle was of a strange shape. No label. Pieces of wood followed. And then a darker shape appeared far away. A rubber dinghy. Drifting out to sea. A man in it. No oars. Trying to row with the palms of his hands. Hopelessly.

Mr Shepherd hurried to the small landing stage on the other side of the Big House, where his boat was. Petrol! So little of it was left and it was so difficult to get more. He started the engine. Had to go round the Island. The man in the dinghy didn't move. Mr Shepherd threw him a rope. The man grasped the end of it but couldn't hold it. The boat moved up and down.

Mr Shepherd was already in his fifties; not sure whether fish was an animal or not, within the meaning of the terms of the Thomas Hobson Agreement, he didn't do any fishing (all fish, already frozen, or smoked, or tinned, was supplied to him – at least in peacetime – from the mainland), and his seamanship was not full of vigour. Thus, it took him a long time to hook the bobbing dinghy in tow and bring it ashore.

The Island's Time was on the grand scale. It marched with steps as long as from sunrise to sunrise. Anything so niggardly short as an hour was too small to meditate upon. The carcase of Matilda, the cow, lay on the grass, in the sunshine. The little boy, Gregory was running in the orchard, now and then glancing at Matilda and quickly turning back to hide behind a tree. In the farmhouse, Mrs Shepherd lay in bed, with the life-greedy little baby Georgina at her breast. Mr Shepherd spread a blanket on the floor of the kitchen, laid the man down gently, covered him with another blanket, put a pillow under his head. Then he sweetened a mug of water with sugar and made him drink it. He sat on the stool beside him and wondered who the man was. And as he wondered, he puzzled . . .

The man in the dinghy was in his underwear. Had he been shipwrecked so unexpectedly that he had had no time to put something on? Or, on the contrary, had he perhaps been in a uniform that he thought it would be safer to throw away, not knowing where the little rubber dinghy would drift him? And then, the rubber dinghy itself. Mr Shepherd didn't think they would have that sort of thing on a big warship, or any ship. An aeroplane – perhaps. But Mr Shepherd knew that he didn't know. That he had no knowledge of that sort of thing. So he just puzzled about it. He got up to cook some pottage. Vegetarian. He came back to the stranger lying on the floor, sat on the stool, lifted the stranger's head with his left hand, and with his right he started to feed him from the spoon. As the stranger opened his mouth, Mr Shepherd found himself thinking, How young the man looked! He couldn't have shaved in his dinghy, of course, and yet he had barely any hair on his beard. He could not have been shipwrecked for very long, or else . . . Was he so young that he didn't need to shave every morning? Still, his body wasn't that of a young boy. On their way from the dinghy to the farmhouse he could scarcely drag himself along, and Mr Shepherd had to keep him from falling, and yet he was not a weakling, his body was mature, but had it matured by age or by hardship, not the hardship of the tennis court but the hardship of life and the vicissitudes of war?

'Do you speak English?' Mr Shepherd asked.

The man didn't answer.

Mr Shepherd opened the door to the bedroom to tell his wife what had happened. But Mrs Shepherd was asleep, and so was the tiny baby girl snuggled up to her. He shut the door. The little boy, Gregory, was standing in the corner of the kitchen, looking at the strange man on the floor. It was the second time in his very long life (more than a thousand days and a thousand nights is a very long time for a child on an island) – it was the second time he had seen a new face; first – it was the face of a little baby girl, his sister, and now – the face of a grown-up man. A face of a grown-up man that was *not* the face of his father.

'Hush . . . Don't wake him up,' his father said.

Some three years back, when the child Gregory was born, Mr and Mrs Shepherd had started to think about his future. The time would come, of course, when the boy would have to be sent to school, if only for a year or two, to Ireland or to England. Before that, however, the boy would have to get some education at home. There were hundreds, well, thousands of books in the Big House's library, but they were books for grown-ups. And so, as the war was just going to start, and they didn't know how long it would last – five years? ten years? – they ordered bottles of ink, steel nibs, pens, pencils, an English primer, and dozens of exercise books. One of those exercise books Mr Shepherd had pinched for himself. Whatever for? He wasn't quite sure. But he felt that he might need it. He felt that he would need it at those very rare moments when his feet, all of a sudden without any warning, took him to the southern tip of the Island, the southernmost tip, where he would sit back on a stone, all alone, and look at the timeless horizon. He thought it was 'melancholy', and he thought that the exercise book would shun melancholy; he thought it would be easy to open a book and write in it words, write words about the greenness of the Island, about the rhythms of the sea, about the ever-changing shapes of the clouded sky. But when he finally put pencil to paper and saw what his hand had written, it surprised him. Because, instead of letting him be when he was, his hand had taken him back, back in time, as if of its own volition. As if of its own volition, it wrote at the top of the page, at the top of the blank page, the first page in the exercise book pinched from his son, as if of its own volition his hand had written at the top of the page the words:

## The English Family Shepherd

*My Father.*

under which, forgetting the greenness of the Island, the movement of the sea, and the clouds of the sky, the hand wrote:

> 'Shepherd was the name of my dad
> But butcher was his job
> His apron was covered in blood
> But he would never sob.
>
>> To eat their meat men will
>> But they are too shy to kill.
>
> So he himself
>> took off their hands
>>> the sin of dirt
> And off their nostrils
>> the smell of blood
> There never ain't a saint
> Who did more for men's soul than my dad.'

No, oh no, that was not at all, not at all, absolutely not at all
what he had wanted to say. He looked at the page as if it
were a strange mirror in which he saw his own face, his own,
yet unknown to him. For a moment, he was tempted to see
more, to learn more. He turned the page of the exercise book
and, on top of the next page he wrote:

*My Mother.*

Then he wrote:

'She

but now he was exhausted. The rest of the page remained blank. And it was still blank, some three years later, when he said, 'Hush, don't wake him up', then left the kitchen and, with the exercise book in his hand, went to the Big House. He spent a long time there, in the reading room, rummaging through the books, especially the foreign language dictionaries, phrase books, guides, making notes on the inner side of the back cover of the exercise book. Back in the farmhouse kitchen, he found the dinghy man sitting on the stool, wrapped up in the blanket, the child on his lap.

'Moo-tilda. Moo moo-tilda,' the child was saying.

Mr Shepherd stopped in front of them and, reading from the exercise book, asked:

'*Sprechen Sie Deutsch?*
'*Parlez-vous français?*
'*Italiano?*
'*Moovee pan po polskoo?*
'*Gahvareetié pa rooskoo?*'

The man didn't answer.

'Deaf?
'*Taub?*
'*Sourd?*
'*Sordo?*
'*Gwoohi?*'

The man didn't answer.

Mr Shepherd started reading again, watching the man carefully after each sentence:

'Wrong in the head?
'*Schwach im Kopf?*
'*Cinglé?*
'*Testa vuota?*
'*Mente cato?*
'*Pomylony?*'

No muscle in the man's face twitched.

Mr Shepherd showed him the inner side of the back cover of the exercise book where the words were written. The man looked at it, but his eyes didn't move.

'Moo . . .' said Greg.

Mr Shepherd made some coffee. Precious wartime coffee. He added a spoonful of precious wartime sweet condensed milk. He gave one mug to the dinghy man, he took the other to his wife.

'What was it?' she asked. 'I thought I heard the sound of a wind and it filled all the house and began to speak with foreign tongues. I slept and must have been full of dreams.'

'It's all right, dear,' he said. 'Everything's all right. Drink your coffee, dear, everything's just fine.'

He went back to the kitchen and told the dinghy man, 'Now, please get it into your head that whoever you are, nobody in this house is your enemy. Or ever will be. All right?'

The dinghy man didn't answer. And he kept being silent for the next forty years.

•

They decided to call him Nemo. Did they know Captain Nemo in Jules Verne's *Twenty Thousand Leagues Under the Sea*? Or of Nemo, the law writer, in Dickens's *Bleak House*? Maybe they had a cousin in a Scottish regiment with *Nemo me impune lacessit* (Nobody provokes me with impunity) embossed around the Order of the Thistle? Or was it the word OMEN spelled backwards, a word allowed in the parlour game during wintery hours in the drawing room of the country house in which Mrs Shepherd was born?

A word not quite suitable for their parlour game was MÉSAL-LIANCE, but this was precisely the word people had on the tip of their tongue when she married the son of a butcher. Which made no difference to her. People, including her family, were somehow neither here nor there in her world. Sort of beyond-her-field-of-vision. She neither liked them nor disliked them. Neither approved nor disapproved. They had their own existence of which she was not part. Well, she was, of course, but not really. *Really* she was part of the existence of the garden and the fields and the wood, she was part of that part of Nature which was neither man nor stones. She had no need for artefacts. Theological artefacts, philosophical artefacts, technological artefacts, social artefacts. They were for her something that had no real, well . . . **no really real existence.** That's how – without passion, without affection – she found it natural that she should live on a minuscule green island surrounded by the grey sea. The only things she missed were the animals. But even Mr Thomas Hobson's contractual clause forbidding the presence of animals on the Island could not get rid of them all, Matilda, the cow, apart, there were birds in the trees, fishes in the sea, caterpillars on the cabbage leaves. And then, there were also two little human creatures which she, herself, had produced. Greg and Georgina. So long as they remained uncontaminated by artefacts, they were just *living creatures*, like animals. And so was the big mute biped who suddenly appeared on the Island out of the grey sea.

His first night on the Island he spent sleeping on the kitchen floor. In the morning he looked completely recovered, and Mr Shepherd took him to the shed where Matilda, the cow, had lived before she died. They cleaned the shed, whitewashed it, and then went to the Big House and from one of the rooms fetched a bed, a mattress, some sheets, and carried them to the shed. That was the second time that Mr Shepherd had taken anything from the Big House. The first time it was the Bible.

'Moo moo,' Greg said.

Mrs Shepherd was still in bed, suckling Georgina, when, through the window, she saw Greg happily riding on Nemo's shoulders.

She sighed.

For lunch they had cucumbers and potatoes, and then an apple pie. After which, Mr Shepherd took Nemo to the field, just beyond the orchard, where the body of Matilda, the cow, was lying on grass.

'Moo moo,' Greg said.

At first, Nemo wasn't sure what he was expected to do. He thought, perhaps, they were going to cut up the carcass, as

99

meat. But they had no hatchets, no choppers, no knives. What they did have was a spade and a shovel. Mr Shepherd started to dig, and Nemo followed. Thus they dug a hole in the ground for Matilda, the cow. After which, Nemo took two twigs, joined them together in the middle with a length of the green tough skin of the stalk, and stuck its end into the mound of earth. That was the first artefact he produced on the island. A theological artefact.

'Moo,' Greg said. 'Moo moo.'

And that was how, in that part of the field, just beyond the orchard, the first cemetery of Hobson's Island acquired its first grave. The next one, many years later, was dug for Mr Shepherd himself.

•

The war was over and half-forgotten. Mr Churchill said: '*[and] so I was immediately dismissed by the British electorate from all further conduct of their affairs*'; Lord Beveridge said: '*the object of government in peace and in war is not the glory of rulers or of races, but the happiness of the common man*'; the children were sent to school, Gregory to Cornwall, Georgina to Ireland. Mr Shepherd didn't know what was the matter with him, and wasn't interested in naming the cause of his illness. All he knew was that he was dying. His voice was weak but very steady when he said to Mrs Shepherd: 'We've had a very good life, my dear, a very good life. And now I'm going to feel weaker and weaker, and that's all for the best. So don't ask me to fight, dear, be glad it's going to end so peacefully. Look after yourself, dear, and don't worry.' He died during the night, in his sleep.

There was no timber suitable for making a coffin. In the basement of the Big House, they (Mrs Shepherd and Nemo) found some empty packing cases. But Mrs Shepherd squirmed at the very thought. And altogether, was a coffin necessary?

Actually, she had never seen a funeral. When her parents died, she was already living on the Island, and she had never left it, even for a day.

Silently, they walked back to that place by the orchard, silently they dug a grave alongside that of Matilda, laid it with moss and twigs, strewed it with evergreen leaves, lined its borders with flowers, and when the shrouded body of Mr Shepherd was lowered down, they heaped some more leaves and twigs, and then some earth on it, and then they sat down on a fallen tree trunk in front of the mound, and – suddenly – Mrs Shepherd realized that – at least, till the children come back from school, Georgina from Ireland, Greg from Cornwall, – she'd have nobody to talk to. She put the palm of her hand on Nemo's knee and kept it there all the time they were sitting on the tree trunk, wordlessly, staring at the mound. And then Nemo stood up and went to his shed. And she got up and went to the farmhouse. And soon the children came back and life on the Island continued, smoothly, except for an occasional gale, or the biennial or triennial visit of Herr Fischer from Switzerland.

By then, little Greg had grown into a young man. He didn't remember Matilda, the cow. He didn't remember that he used to call her 'Moo Moo-tilda'. Surprisingly, Georgina was quite convinced that *she* remembered her, which was quite imposs-ible, because Georgina was born on the day Matilda, the cow, died. 'Of course I remember Matilda,' and she would describe her, and Mrs Shepherd would say, 'Yes, she was white with a black patch between her horns, and black socks on her feet, as you say, and she had a way of turning her head towards me and looking at me with her lovely big eyes, but you couldn't have seen her, you must have heard me, or your father, talking about her.'

'All right, mother. So I have never seen her,' Georgina would say; still – she was not convinced.

There was quite a number of things which she knew were

true as facts, yet she wasn't quite convinced that they were really true. One of them was Nemo. She couldn't believe that Nemo had appeared on the Island on the day Matilda died and she, Georgina, was born. For her, Nemo had been an integral part of the Island since the beginning of the world. He had the Island's wordless silence and the Island's smell. He was, and must have ever been, the Island. Her brother, Greg, felt the same. He was only three when Nemo appeared and he couldn't remember the Island without Nemo. What he and his sister remembered was how they rode happily on Nemo's shoulders, how Nemo taught them to climb trees, to burrow into the earth, to watch the sky, to swim in the sea. Wordlessly. Always. They had learned millions of things from him, none of them being given a name. Their parents would tell them what to do and what not to do. But the real, the ' "Why?"-less' knowledge of what one does and what one doesn't, they had received from Nemo. Without a word. Without a gesture.

That kind of not-at-all verbal knowledge of the world and its ways was something special, something that made them feel different from the other boys and girls whom they met when they were sent to school. Greg to Cornwall. Georgina to Ireland. They treasured that 'something' that set them apart, they were proud of it, it made them feel superior, especially on those occasions when they were jeered at by other boys and girls for whom they were strangers coming from nowhere. 'Where do you come from?' Georgina, who was at school in Ireland, would say: 'Cornwall'. Gregory, who was at school in Cornwall, would say: 'Cork'. They would never mention their Island. The Island was something wordless, not express-ible in profane gabble. The world of gabble and the world of Nemo were two separate worlds. It was in the world of gabble that they learned about sex. In the school lavatories, mostly. Described in four-letter terms. But, in their minds, what they learned had nothing to do with Georgina's monthly periods, or with Gregory's wet-dream pollutions. To the world of gabble, the schoolroom 1+1=2 also belonged, as the point of departure to the whole universe of mathematical logic. This 1+1=2 seemed all right to them just so long as it had no bearing on life, so long as they didn't ask *1+1 of what?* and *when?* Because one snowflake + one snowflake are not two snowflakes if the sun melts them before you have had time to find the answer. And one egg + one egg is not exactly the same as two eggs if one of them is a cuckoo's egg, just being hatched. And one human being + one human being make an entirely different sum if it is Mr Shepherd + Mrs Shepherd, and not Mr Shepherd + Mr Fischer, or Mr Fischer + Nemo, or Nemo + Mrs Shepherd, or Mrs Shepherd + Mr Fischer, or Nemo + Mr Shepherd. Georgina was quite happy at her school in Ireland, actually, and Greg was quite happy at his school in Cornwall, but when, after two terms, they came back to Hobson's Island, they wouldn't go to school again, no, please, never again.

•

When Gregory was twenty-one and Georgina no longer a child, Mrs Shepherd arranged with the bank in Cornwall and the bank in Cork to transfer her (and her late husband's) joint accounts into the children's names. As it would be much easier to send a letter to Antipodes Island (50 South 175 East) than to Hobson's Island (50 North 5 West or about), the formalities took a long time. She waited patiently. The day she learnt that this had been done, she went to her bedroom and shut the door. There she spent (most of the time in bed) the whole winter. Hibernating. The children thought that when the spring came she would be her old self again. She wasn't. A doctor fetched by Georgina was angry. She actually kidnapped him. He wasn't told how far Hobson's Island was. He looked at Mrs Shepherd and said, 'Hospital!' And asked to be taken back to the civilized world. 'Hospital? You don't mean it,' Mrs Shepherd said. They didn't. Nemo boiled some leaves, some small white flowers and berries and roots, and gave her spoonfuls of the brew to make the pain easier to bear.

The next time Georgina took the boat, it was to buy a coffin. They buried Mrs Shepherd alongside the other two graves. The flyleaf of the Bible (the Bible none of them had ever read) had to be turned over to register the event on it.

•

By the end of the next spring, a Herr Braun appeared on the island.

'Herr Fischer has retired. So now I am your *comptroller*, yes?'

Gregory didn't like the word. 'Did you have a good crossing?' he asked.

'What? Oh, yes. Thank you,' Herr Braun said.

'This is Herr Braun. This is my sister Georgina,' Gregory said.

'Pleased to meet you, miss,' Herr Braun said. 'And may I see your mother?'

They took him to the place beyond the orchard.

'This is Mother's. That is Father's. And that is Matilda's,' they said.

'Matilda? Who was Matilda?' Herr Braun asked.

'Matilda, the cow,' Gregory said.

'The cow? *Die Kuh?*' Herr Braun asked.

'Yes.'

'How come? You know animals are not allowed on the Island, don't you?'

'Yes, I do,' Gregory said. 'But I don't know why. Can you tell me?'

'No,' Herr Braun said. 'And it was I who asked you the question.'

'What question?'

'How did it happen that a cow was here?'

'Matilda was an exception. Herr Fischer knew about her. And, before him, Herr Schmied knew about her.'

'They did?'

'Yes,' Gregory said. And he was sure now that Herr Braun also knew and was trying to learn more by pretending ignorance. This must have been his method . . .

'And who is that man?' Herr Braun asked, pointing at Nemo.

'He's our gardener,' Gregory said.

'*Guten Tag*, Herr Gärtner,' Herr Braun said.

'Why do you address him in German?' Gregory asked.

'I really have no idea,' Herr Braun said.

'Anyway, he's deaf and dumb,' Gregory said.

'Oh, is he?' Herr Braun said.

'Would you like me to make some coffee, Herr Braun?' Georgina said.

'Yes please, my dear,' Herr Braun said. 'Perhaps a bit later. Now, I should like your brother to show me his Island.'

'What would you like to see?' Gregory asked.

'Everything,' said Herr Braun and started walking southward.

There was the sea, no more than half a mile on their left, and there was the sea, no more than half a mile on their right. As they walked, they could see it on their left and on their right, between the trunks of the trees that seemed to be passing them by. Herr Braun measured his steps cautiously so as not to tread on the flowers. But there were too many of them, pale blue and silvery grey, pure white and deep purple, orange-red and bright yellow, among the green blades and broad leaves, and prickle-toothed leaves of the grasses and the shrubbery, and above them were the bees buzzing from flower to flower, and a bumble-bee assaulting the sun-reflecting radiance of Mr Braun's patent-leather shoes.

'Do you have your own honey?' he asked.

'Oh yes,' Gregory said. 'Would you like to take a jar as a present for Herr Fischer? And accept one for yourself perhaps? Shall I ask Georgina to prepare them?'

'*Sic vos non vobis mellificatis apes,*' Herr Braun quoted.

'I beg your pardon?' Gregory said.

' "Thus, not for yourselves you bees make your honey",' Herr Braun translated, and Gregory didn't learn whether to ask Georgina or not.

They walked in silence till they came to the very tip of the Island. That was the very same place where Gregory's father, Mr Shepherd, used to go on those rare occasions when melancholy caught him. The same spot where, twenty years back, he had opened the exercise book and written that poem about his own father, the butcher. Herr Braun spread a handkerchief on a large sun-warmed piece of rock and sat down. There was the sea on their left, the sea on their right, and the sea just in front of them, bursting at their feet and boundless at the horizon where its colour was the colour of the sky.

'*Wunderbar!*' Herr Braun said. 'Such majesty! One doesn't need to go to church . . . To be overwhelmed . . . *Je te salue! Vieil océan!* . . . Only to think that you can come to this place every day, my friend! . . . I don't know . . . Perhaps I envy you . . . Perhaps I don't . . . I don't know . . . Do you?'

'Do I what?' Gregory asked.

'Do you come to this place often, to sit here, to contemplate its grandeur, the Grandeur of God? In whose will is our peace,' Herr Braun said. And added, '*E'n la sua volontade è nostra pace.*'

That was not a way of talking Gregory was used to. The words were beautiful. The sound of the words was beautiful and it made him feel frightened. He never heard such words spoken, except on the radio. Where they were impersonal, mechanical, as if they were spoken by the loudspeaker. But here they were spoken by a real man, who was sitting beside him, a real man, not shying away from using such unnatural language, a banker from Switzerland who calls himself his, Gregory's, *comptroller*!

'*Nun*, my friend,' Herr Braun said, 'don't you wish to tell me of yourself . . . ?'

'What do you want to know, Herr Braun?'

'Well, my friend. Your dear parents are no longer. So you are the master now. It's a great responsibility, isn't it?'

'It's all right, Herr Braun.'

'Well, so that's fine. For the time being. But surely you must be having some plans for the future, mustn't you?'

'Must I?'

'Well, my friend, you are young. You may want to go, see the world, *ja?*'

'No, I don't,' Gregory said.

'You want to stay here, on this lonely island?!'

'I don't feel lonely,' Gregory said.

'Perhaps not yet, my friend, but you will, you will. You will need company. The company of a woman. A wife . . .'

'That's all right, Herr Braun. I have a fiancée and I am going to marry her.'

'You have? That's marvellous, my friend.' He took a cigar from a cigar-case, and a cigar-cutter, and a little box of matches. 'You do not smoke, do you?'

'No, I don't,' Gregory said.

'Very wise, my friend, very wise.' A puff of cigar smoke sweetened the breeze blowing from the sea. 'And the lady . . . Your fiancée . . . How old is she?'

'She's two years younger . . .'

'And does she know about the Island? Has she seen it? Is she prepared to live here?'

'Oh yes,' Gregory said.

'Well, so I congratulate you, my friend,' he puffed at his cigar, and then asked: 'Does the lady come from Ireland or from England?'

'Cornwall,' Gregory said.

'And her name is . . . ?'

'. . . Geraldine,' Gregory said.

'Geraldine what?'

'Geraldine Sss . . . stubbs.'

Herr Braun was silent for a little time. Till his silence was confused by the sound of the sea. Then, as if there had been nothing curious about the pause, he looked up and spoke in his ordinary tone of voice:

'On our way back, I'd like you to show me the house.'

'The Big House?'

'Is that what you call it?'

'Yes.'

'I want you to show me the Big House.'

'Nothing has changed there, we just keep it clean. We are not using it,' Gregory said.

'Of course you are *not*,' Herr Braun said.

'Except the library,' Gregory said. 'We read the books. That's all right, isn't it?'

'*Ja, ja.* I don't see why not,' Herr Braun said. And then he asked, 'Look, my friend, did your father or your mother tell you about the articles of the agreement?'

'About what?' Gregory asked.

'About the contract of the employment. The rules. What you can do, and still more, what you cannot.'

'No,' Gregory said. 'Not really. I just know those things naturally. Because I live here.'

'*So* . . . And nothing puzzles you about the rules?'

'Oh yes,' Gregory said. 'For instance – animals. Why – no animals? Not even a dog. I'd like to have a dog. Nobody would kill a dog, would they?'

'No. Unless one has a bitch who has too many puppies.'

'I've never thought that way,' Gregory said.

'Well, my friend, you do not need to think, that's to say, you do not need to think further back than the rules. The rules are where the buck starts from. For you as well as for us, the lawyers. It's like with the Commandments. Everything that precedes them is metaphysics. And we are not interested in metaphysics, are we?' He paused; and then, all of a sudden, he asked sharply, 'Has anybody been visiting the Island lately?'

'Oh, no,' Gregory said.

'Think harder,' Herr Braun said.

'Well, I mean nobody, except for the fishermen delivering things from the shops, and – yes – the doctor who came to see Mother, he stayed here no more than an hour, he didn't want to come, my sister practically kidnapped him . . .' Gregory said.

Herr Braun eyed him sternly.

'Nobody else?'

'No.'

'You must have forgotten your fiancée, my friend. Didn't you say that she had been here?'

Gregory blushed and said nothing.

'Well, never mind,' Herr Braun pressed the lit end of the cigar against the rock, looked at it, and then threw it into the sea. The breeze threw it back and it landed at his feet. 'What I want to know is: Has anybody been here to inquire about the Big House? Especially, anybody from London?'

'No, sir.'

'You are positive?'

'Yes, sir.'

'And the fact doesn't worry you? Doesn't intrigue you?'

'Why should it?'

'Well, what about all those electronic gadgets stored under the roof of the Big House?'

'They've been there since before I was born, sir.'

'Precisely. Since the beginning of the war. Which is quite a long time, isn't it? And that obsolete junk is still there. And London people are still paying you one pound every week.

You don't think they do so because somebody there might have forgotten to countermand the order to pay, or do you?'

'I don't know,' Gregory said. 'And if it is a question of money . . .'

'No,' Herr Braun interrupted him, 'it is not a question of money. It is something quite different.' He stopped for a moment, and then asked, 'Now, tell me, do you know what a "safe house" is?'

'I'm not sure,' Gregory said.

'It is a place where it is safe to hide a person. A foreign agent, a dissident, a supergrass, a deposed monarch. I'm telling you that, my friend, so that you would know what it is all about when they come to you and say: Somebody has been ill and needs sea air to recover; could you take care of him for a few weeks till he's well enough to get back into circulation. Or, there is a writer who needs some solitude to finish his book, can you board him for a while, but don't let him use your boat. Well, my friend, something like that is likely to happen. And, sooner or later, it will happen. Maybe tomorrow, maybe in ten years, maybe in twenty. But it is bound to happen. The British don't pay one pound a week for nothing.'

'And when they come, you want me to refuse . . .' Gregory said.

'On the contrary, my friend. I want you to accept. You see, this island is very vulnerable. You have no police force. You have no army. Anybody who knows about you, can invade you. And so your best defence is – not to be known. And to be treated as a safe house by a secret service will help you to be unknown.'

'Are you secret service, sir?'

'*Himmel!*' Herr Braun exclaimed. 'Would I have told you if I were? No! But, *Gott sei Dank!* I'm not. I am a Gnome of Zürich. I know things because I observe the chessboard. But I don't play, myself. I'm not even interested in the players.

What I am interested in is the Kings and the Queens, the Bishops, the Knights, the Rooks of all kinds, and, first of all, the pawns. And the chessboard of this beautiful God's earth!' He stood up, and turned round. '*O, wunderschön ist Gottes Erde,*' he said. Then he stooped a little, as if with old age . . . 'Look at this, my friend,' he said, 'its proper name is *narcissus poeticus*! Look at the sheer beauty of it. There are philosophers who think that such beauty must have been designed. Therefore it, the beauty of it, is the proof of the existence of God. And yet, it is so vulnerable! This poor *narcissus poeticus* is. If I put down my foot, my patent-leather shoe could smash it without any effort at all.'

'Please, Herr Braun, don't,' Gregory said.

'Of course not,' Herr Braun said. And added, 'I wish Time were as sentimental as the sole of my shoe is.' He smiled. And then said briskly, 'Incidentally, I haven't yet answered your question. The answer is: Yes, of course, please ask your sister to be so kind as to prepare two jars of honey. One for Herr Fischer and one for myself. My wife will be very pleased. Her name is Helga. You can write on the label: *to Frau Helga Braun*. And now let us go and have a look at the Big House.'

•

Two weeks later, when the fisherman from Ireland came with the usual delivery of sugar, coffee, flour, aspirin, toilet rolls and whatnot, Georgina packed her suitcase and asked him to take her across. She winked at her brother, winked at Nemo, and winked at the fisherman. Those were three winks and they had three different meanings. When, bobbing on the water, the fisherman asked her, 'Will you be coming back soon, Miss?' she said, 'Not bloody likely. You don't think I want to spend all my life on that bloody island, do you?'

Put ashore at Cork harbour, she went straight to her bank, cashed a big sum of money from her and her brother's joint account, and took the train to Dublin. From Dublin she went to Belfast, and from there (Belfast Donegal Quay) she took a night ferry to Liverpool (Princes Dock). In Liverpool she went to the tourist office and asked for the address of a boarding house in London. They thought she was a student and recommended one on the outskirts of Bloomsbury. She bought an envelope, wrote on it *To Miss Geraldine Stubbs* and posted it to the boarding house address. Then, from Liverpool (Lime Street) she took the train to London (Euston). She was lucky, they had a room for her in the boarding house. Next morning she received the envelope she had posted from Liverpool, she tore it open and put it into her handbag. She had never been in London before, yet she had no difficulty in finding her way. She went to a public library and said she wanted to borrow books. They asked her for her name and address and she showed them the envelope. In those years, in London, people who had no reason not to believe you, believed you. They gave her a little card on which they wrote: *Geraldine Stubbs*, and the address in Bloomsbury. 'You can take three books and keep them for a fortnight,' they told her. 'Thank you,' she said, 'I'll come back to choose.' From the library she went to a post office. Could she start a Post Office Savings Book with just five pounds? 'You can, love,' they said. 'What's your name?' She fumbled in her handbag and took out the envelope, the library card, and five single pound notes. 'You must wait a little, love,' they said and gave her a form to sign. She signed: *Geraldine Stubbs*. Thus, she now had three pieces of 'identification': the envelope, the library card, and the Post Office book. In the afternoon, she went to a hairdresser, she knew exactly how she wanted her hair done, and what kind of make-up to buy. When she came back to the boarding house, they didn't recognize her at first, and then said she looked so lovely. Next morning she went shopping. A new suitcase, new handbag, skirts, blouses, jackets, trouser suit, jeans, underwear, nightgown, high-heeled shoes. Back in the boarding house, she took a bath, transferred things from the old handbag to the new one, put everything old, including the handbag and the shoes, into the old suitcase, put on the new clothes, took the old suitcase with her and went down. 'Are you leaving us already?' they asked. 'No, I'll be coming back.' They shouldn't worry. She had paid for the whole week in advance. She went to the Euston Station tearoom, put the old suitcase under the table, and ordered tea. When she left the station without the suitcase, she hoped that somebody would steal it, or else that they'd send it to the lost property stores, or Oxfam.

In the evening, she went to the theatre. At school, she had taken part in amateur theatricals, but she had never before been in a real theatre. She was now sitting in the middle of the front stalls, seeing the stage very clearly, hearing every word very clearly, but her mind was closed to what she so clearly saw and heard. She wondered why. As she had been used to listening to plays on the radio, she tried to shut her eyes and take in only the words. It didn't help. Preoccupied with those of its own, her mind was sealed to the plans, plots, problems of those alien people who made so much fuss about themselves in the play. When, later on, she was asked what she had seen, she couldn't remember. She said, 'Oh, something, you know . . . well, never mind.'

The next day she did some more shopping (a magnum bottle of champagne, among other things) and, in the evening, she took a taxi to Paddington Station, and from there the midnight sleeper to Penzance (Cornwall). She decided not to show herself to the people who were making their regular deliveries to Hobson's Island; instead, she boarded a helicopter which, in twenty minutes, took her from Penzance Heliport to St Mary's Airport in the Isles of Scilly, where, she hoped, she'd find a motorboat to take her to Hobson's Island. She did. The boat belonged to a Mr Wilkinson. 'Hobson's Island?' he said. 'Never heard of it!' 'Never mind,' she retorted. 'I can steer you to it with my eyes closed.' They arrived late in the evening, later than Mr Wilkinson expected, but his good humour sparkled when they invited him to dinner and he saw the magnum bottle of champagne (which he called 'bubbly').

Gregory and Geraldine (that's how Georgina will be called now) had never drunk champagne in their lives, and they had just found that a little of it was more than enough for them. Nemo didn't drink at all. And so most of the magnum was imbibed by Mr Wilkinson, who became gayer and gayer, especially when he started to lace it with a little of the brandy he poured out of the small flat-sided, leather-covered flask he carried in his hip pocket.

'Hope you've guessed, Wilkinson, that this feast is our wedding feast,'

'Is it? Didn't know you were married, old boy,' Wilkinson said.

'We are not. We are going to be,' Gregory said.

'Putting the cart before the horse, old boy? Most irregular. Yes. Most irregular. Congratulations, anyway. And best wishes to the lady, I'm sure. When is it going to take place, old man?'

'Tonight. At midnight,' Gregory said.

'Most irregular. Most irregular, old boy. Still . . . *in articulo mortis* everything's possible. Are you dying, old boy, or something?'

'Not in the least,' Gregory said.

'Most irregular,' Mr Wilkinson repeated, 'to have done it *in articulo mortis* and refuse to die – is most irregular. Still . . . *in extremis* can be stretched to include more than is strictly regular . . . Well, suppose you are *in extremis*, meaning you're in extreme difficulties, though not necessarily at your last gasp. So be it. *Fac et excusa*, meaning fuck and apologize later. OK. Now, who's going to marry you, old boy?'

'You,' Gregory said.

'Me?' Mr Wilkinson said.

114

'Yes, you,' Gregory said.

''Twasn't included in my fee,' Mr Wilkinson said.

'We'll double your fee,' Gregory said.

'Well, for treble the fee, I'll do anything in the name of the Old Harry,' Mr Wilkinson said.

'I said double, not treble,' Gregory said.

'*Fiat voluntas tua*,' said Mr Wilkinson.

'Actually, we don't need any Latin,' Gregory said. 'And actually, he's a priest,' he pointed at Nemo. 'But he's dumb, actually . . .'

'On a desert island even a dumb man is a preacher,' Mr Wilkinson said.

'So, you see, he'll bless us, but it's you who'll be doing all the talking. In plain English. No Latin.'

'A dumb preacher . . .' Mr Wilkinson repeated. 'Most irregular. I say, is he both dumb and deaf?'

'Yes. But he understands everything,' Gregory said.

'He does? How does he do it?' Mr Wilkinson asked.

'Because he loves us,' Geraldine said.

'Does he?' Mr Wilkinson said. 'Of course he does. And so do I. You're a nice couple, you two. A lovely couple. You look like twins, did you know that? Like brother and sister. Most irregular,' Mr Wilkinson said.

'Oh, shut up,' Gregory said.

'Now, old boy,' Mr Wilkinson said. 'I don't know what got into you to say a thing like that to me. Who do you think Adam's sons slept with if not with their sisters? Or mother? And daughters and nieces? Most irregular for God Almighty to start the pro-lif-er-ation of Mankind in that sort of way, if you ask me. Most irregular!' He stood up and, addressing Gregory, said, 'Let there be no strife, I pray thee, between thee and me, for we be brethren.' He raised his glass and, swaying a little, continued, 'Here's to the bride and bride-groom!' He drank slowly, solemnly, then he put the glass down on the table, punctiliously, and said, 'Now, let's go to the bedroom, and I'll marry you in front of the Altar of Love.'

'Steady, old man!' Gregory said. 'You need some fresh air. We all need some fresh air. Let's totter out and have a breather.'

The midnight sky was cloudless, lit by the shine of the Milky Way and the rising moon. Somewhere, among the stars, the winking eye of a passing aeroplane moved leisurely westwards. Mr Wilkinson stood erect at the water's edge, sternly faced the sea, and addressed the incoming waves thus: 'If any of you, my Waves, know cause, or just impediment, why these two persons should not be joined together in holy Matrimony, ye are to declare it. This is the first time of asking.'

He waited till the second ridge of water curled over and broke on the shore, and said: 'This is the second time of asking.'

Then, as the third ridge of water curled over and broke on the shore, he concluded: 'This is the third time of asking.'

He waited again, and – as no beachcomber came rolling in from the sea, and no great wave leapt at the headland to declare an objection – he turned to Nemo, and said, 'Dearly beloved, if any man can shew any just cause, why they may not lawfully be joined together, let him speak, or else hereafter for ever hold his peace!'

Nemo held his peace and said nothing.

Then Mr Wilkinson turned to Gregory.

'Treble fee?' he asked.

'No,' Gregory said. 'Double.'

'Then I'll give you a quickie.'

'All right.'

'Gregory, wilt thou have this Woman to thy wedded wife, et cetera, et cetera, et cetera?'

'I will.'

'That's what I feared you would say, lucky boy!' Mr Wilkinson grunted. And turned to Geraldine.

116

'Geraldine, do you really want to marry that man, to satisfy his carnal lusts and appetites, like brute beasts that have no understanding?'

'I do,' Geraldine said.

'Are you sure?'

'I am.'

'Wouldn't you rather have me?'

'No,' she said.

'Well, so that's that,' Mr Wilkinson said. 'I pronounce that you be Man and Wife together.'

'What about the ring?' Geraldine asked.

'Oh, how fussy you are, my dear,' Mr Wilkinson said. 'You give it to him yourself. Poor Man was born free, and everywhere he ends with a ring at the end of his nose. Tàm Tàm taRàmtam Tàmtam, Tàratàra Tàm Tàm taRàm Tàm . . .' he sang, as he marched, wobbly on his legs, back to the farmhouse.

They sat round the table. Gregory fetched the Bible and opened it on the flyleaf, where, *recto*, recorded was the birth of himself; and the death of Matilda, the cow; and the birth of Georgina; and the appearance of Nemo; and the death of Mr Shepherd; and, *verso*, the death of Mrs Shepherd.

'You write it down, Wilkinson,' Gregory said.

'Write what?'

'You write the date first. Then you write: *The Marriage took place*, then you write: *of Mr Gregory Shepherd to Miss Geraldine Stubbs*, and then you sign it.'

He did. And signed it: *I. K. Wilkinson SJ.*

'He should sign it too,' he said, pointing to Nemo.

'He can't, he hasn't got a name,' Gregory said. And then, looking at Mr Wilkinson's signature, he asked, 'And what do the letters "SJ" stand for?'

Mr Wilkinson took the flask out of his hip-pocket. But it was empty. So he only sniffed at it. And then, after a long while, said, 'So you didn't know that you were married by a real padre? A lapsed padre but still a padre. A POW padre. The King gave him a Distinguished Service Medal, and the Pope unfrocked him. Because he fell from grace. And he fell from grace because, after he had seen what he had seen, in 1942 to 45 in Java, instead of blaming the Japs, he blamed God. Ha!' He snorted. 'And now, your unfrocked POW padre is a Scilly Islands *gondoliere!*' He started to sing: '*O sole mio, Santa Loo-oo-ci-ah* . . . ' He tried to get up, and collapsed. Upon which, Gregory and Nemo carried him to bed.

Next morning he woke up, cheerful and happy, no hangover, but he didn't remember a thing, except – vaguely – that there had been some heavy drinking, hadn't there? When they were paying him, he said, 'That's a lot of money. Are you sure it's all right with you?' When they were passing by the Big House, he asked, 'Anybody live there?' When they said, 'No,' he said, 'Must be haunted.' And when they came down to the jetty where his boat was, he said, 'Amazing! I'm not quite sure where I am actually. How do I go from here?'

'Cork is North, Land's End is East. With this clear weather, if you go East by South, you'll soon see your Scillies on the horizon,' Geraldine said.

'Good . . .' he said. 'Well, if you ever come to my island, be my guests. Harold Wilson, you know, is my neighbour. And his wife, Mary. Maybe I can introduce you. He's the best Labour Prime Minister we Conservatives have ever had. Smokes a pipe and you can meet him in the pub. And she writes poetry. They both like poetry. He likes a Psalm by Longfellow, and she likes a fellow called Henry Vaughan. Most regular, both of them are. He likes something about the Soul, and she likes something about the Soul. He likes:

> 'Tell me not, in mournful numbers,
>     "Life is but an empty dream!"
> For the soul is dead that slumbers,
>     And things are not what they seem.'

'And she likes:

> My soul, there is a country
> Far beyond the stars,
> Where stands a wingèd sentry
> All skilful in the wars:

'Most regular stanzas, most regular stanzas indeed. And he, you see, he likes to tell people what to do, and she likes to tell people what to do. He tells them:

> Let us, then, be up and doing,
> With a heart for any fate;
> Still achieving, still pursuing,
> Learn to labour and to wait.

'And she tells them:

> Leave then thy foolish ranges;
> For none can thee secure
> But One who never changes –
> Thy God, thy life, thy cure.

'OK,' Mr Wilkinson snorted, ' "fate-wait, secure-cure", well, dears, tell that to the marines,' and then (as if the echo of the previous night's drinking had reverberated in his brain) he added,'. . . to those POW ones, who didn't disembowel themselves to satisfy the Japs' idea of honour.'

He looked so puzzled at what he had said, as if he didn't know why he had . . . Then he turned to Gregory, and asked in his ordinary tone of voice, 'Tell me, old boy, if you don't mind, who is that deaf and dumb fellow you call Nemo, where does he come from?'

'I don't know,' Gregory said. 'Nobody knows. It was during the war. My father rescued him, as he was drifting in a rubber dinghy, half-naked and half-alive. He has never said a word to anybody.'

'That's exactly the kind of thing I thought it might be,' Mr

Wilkinson said. 'You know, Gregory, old boy, I don't believe he's deaf and dumb. I've seen cases like that, indeed I have. *In periculo maris*, in danger from the sea, when they come face to face with death, they say, "Oh, God, if You save me, I'll give up smoking and drinking", or: "I'll never go to bed with a woman", or "a man", as the case may be, or "I vow perpetual silence, I vow never to speak again", as, I think, might be what happened to your Nemo.' He paused, and then added: 'If I were you, I wouldn't let him think that you know . . .'

There was another pause, and then Geraldine said: 'Do you have enough fuel, Mr Wilkinson?'

'I love you, Miss Stubbs, for asking me that question,' Mr Wilkinson said. 'For thinking about it. You are a real woman. Yes, I'm sure I have. All the same, thank you.'

When Mr Wilkinson left, Geraldine said, 'I've seen too many people these last few days, I don't want to see anybody any more till the end of my life.'

And so life on the Island weaved on through the pattern of one set of four seasons following another. After two years, Geraldine gave birth to a little girl they decided to call Louise. A year later, another girl – Jane. And after two more years, a boy – Philip.

Louise was eighteen, Jane seventeen, and Philip fifteen, when (as Herr Braun had predicted some twenty years before) a message came:

*From the desk of*: LUCY
Mr and Mrs Shepherd will soon be requested to give board and lodging to a v. distinguished gentleman (black). Details will follow.

# PART TWO

## FIVE

*. . . start from the beginning . . .*

The doorbell rang once; briefly. Or did it? He was not quite sure. Not long before, he thought he had heard a flock of birds singing beautifully. But it was in the middle of a dark night when only owls would have hooted or a frightened little mouse squeaked. Then the bell rang again, and he went to open the door. A woman with a suitcase. She stood so close to the door that when he opened it she nearly burst in.

'Mr Sean D'Earth?' she asked.

'Yes . . .'

'You are Adam D'Earth's father?'

'That's right.'

'Please shut the door, I don't want them to see me,' she said.

He looked out. There was nobody in the street. He closed the door. 'Do come in,' he said.

In the hall, she put the suitcase down, and said,'I want to die.'

'We all do,' Sean D'Earth said.

'So why don't we?' she asked.

'Because of the body. The mystery of the body. Or the chemistry of the body. Or both.'

He wanted to ask her who she was. And – first of all – what she knew about his son, Adam. But, as he looked at her face, he decided to wait. He helped her with her overcoat, took her to the room, and sat her in an armchair.

'He asked me to go and see you,' she said. 'The boat that brought him was still waiting for him there, and he asked me to go. To London. He gave me your address and said, "Go, go to London, go to see my father, and tell him that I am sorry. Yes, go, and tell him that he was right, that he had always been right, and that I am sorry," that's what he said to me. That's exactly what he said, that you were right and that he was sorry.'

'Where was that?' Sean asked.

'Where? There, of course. On the Island.'

'Which island?' Sean asked.

'*My* island, Hobson's Island!'

'Is he still there?'

'Who?' she asked.

'My son. Adam.'

'I'm sure he is,' she said.

'Doing what?'

She didn't answer.

'What does he do there?' he repeated.

'He laughs,' she said, looking straight at him.

'He does what?!'

'He laughs! Laughs!'

She buried her face in her hands.

'Is his wife, and his daughter, with him? Is Lucy there? And Deborah?'

She didn't answer.

Now, slowly, some bits of the picture started falling into place. When was it? Just a few days . . . Three? Four? No, not as long as five days ago, the telephone had woken him very early in the morning. It was Adam. Both anxious and irritated. 'Father?'; 'Yes . . .'; 'Is Lucy there, with you?'; 'No, should she be?'; 'Is Deborah?'; 'No, why . . . ?'; 'They've disappeared, that's why. You wouldn't know where they are, Father, would you?'; 'No, I'm afraid not; no, but tell me . . .'; 'Oh.' He had put the receiver down. And that was that. No, it wasn't. Well, not exactly. Didn't he, Sean, when Adam came to see him the other day, hadn't he omitted to tell him (for some trifling reason, so trifling that he didn't even remember now what it was) well, anyway, hadn't he omitted to tell Adam that he had seen Deborah? And what if what Deborah had told him, oh gosh, what if it was of some importance now . . . He dialled his son's telephone number and said, 'Adam, listen, when I saw Deborah not long ago, by chance, at the Serpentine Gallery, Kensington Gardens, she told me that Lucy was going on one of her hush-hush escapades and wanted to take her, yes, to take Deborah, with her. No, she didn't tell me where to, I don't think she knew, she just mentioned an island. What? I think she said a desert island. No, it couldn't possibly be so very far because they were to go there by helicopter. No, I don't know where from, she didn't tell me, but I assumed somehow, perhaps wrongly, that it was from Cornwall'; 'Oh hell! Oh God Almighty!' Adam said. 'But you know her boss. Why couldn't you ask him'; 'I'm going to,' Adam said. 'And if it is what I hope it isn't, I'll kill him!' He slammed down the receiver. And that was that. Lucy had her hush-hush job and Adam had his hush-hush job, and now it seemed that the two had clashed and the result was sitting there, in Sean's armchair, burying her face in her hands.

'I think you need a drink,' he said. 'Let me give you a drop of brandy.'

She lifted her head and said, 'I don't drink. The last time I had a drink . . . it was twenty years ago . . . champagne . . . a magnum bottle, most of which was drunk by a defrocked padre who became a boatman and, one midnight, married me to my brother Gregory. So, you see, I am both Miss Shepherd and Mrs Shepherd, Miss Georgina Shepherd and Mrs Geraldine Shepherd, you may call me whichever you wish, I am both, I am two in one, I am . . .' She stopped abruptly, and laughed, but her laughter, if it was laughter, lasted such a short fraction of a second that it sounded more like a hiccup.

'Well,' he said. 'So you don't drink. But you must eat. Have you had any breakfast?'

He went to the kitchen, poured three cups of cold water into a saucepan, added a teaspoonful of salt, took a dry cup, filled it with porridge oats and started stirring it into the saucepan. While bringing it to the boil and still stirring, he wondered what he should call her, Miss? Mrs? Geraldine? Georgina? Did she really mean she was married to her brother? While the porridge was simmering (four minutes) and the kettle boiling, he started making coffee and tried to concentrate on cooking. He broke two eggs into a bowl to scramble them, then he added another egg, perhaps he'd eat some too, why not? He had already had his breakfast, all alone, at dawn, as every morning, and then went back to bed, but, for a change, it would be nice to have company, so he'd have another breakfast, *en deux*, with this unexpected visitor. He opened the door and said, 'Breakfast is ready.'

But she said, 'May I go to the bathroom?'

He said, 'Yes, of course,' but immediately added 'Wait a second, please,' and he himself went to the bathroom first.

There was a little hook for fastening the door, a little hook and a little ring screwed to the doorframe. He unscrewed the little ring and put it in his pocket. So that she couldn't lock herself in. Hadn't she said that she wanted to die? Well, he didn't want her to do anything silly in his bathroom. He went out and she went in. But he remained standing behind the closed unlocked door. He thought about the lost breakfast *en deux*, about the congealed porridge, cold coffee – it was fortunate he hadn't cooked the eggs he had already scrambled – good, thinking of porridge, coffee, eggs, was better than thinking of . . . 'Are you all right?' he asked after a few minutes. 'Breakfast is getting cold.'

She opened the door. 'No, I don't want any food,' she said. 'What I would like is to have a bath, may I? I haven't even washed for a long time, two days, three days, since I left Ireland to go back to the Island, and then left the Island in a hurry to come here . . .' She started undressing. 'No, don't

126

go. Don't leave me alone. I don't want to be alone. Do sit down. There. On the Island we always swam naked, Gregory and the children, and our parents when they were alive, and Nemo. He was teaching us to swim, all of us . . .'

'Who was Nemo?' Sean asked.

'He was an old man, well, younger than you are, but he was as old as the Island, he was part of the Island, Oh God, why do I say he was, he is, is, *is!*'

'Your bath is ready,' he said, turning the taps off. Then he sat on the cover of the lavatory seat and asked, 'Do you really want me to stay?'

She said, 'Yes.'

Her full frontal nudity was facing him now, but there was a mirror behind her, and in the mirror he saw a large birthmark – or was it a wart? – on the small of her back. It embarrassed him, the fact that he had noticed it, embarrassed him, and his eyes shifted, but she didn't know about the mirror, she only saw that his eyes had now focused on her belly, and she misread his thoughts, and touching it with her finger, she said, 'I know what you think, you think that I am pregnant, yes, you're right, I am, that's why I wanted to die and – at the same time – that's what keeps me going; two opposite things, can you understand that? Yes, *you* can. You said it's the mystery of the body, or the chemistry of the body, or both!'

The bath salts made the water green and scented. She didn't relax, she curled in it. As on a sofa. 'There is nothing one can do,' she said. 'There is absolutely nothing one can do. One can do nothing. Nothing. Even to find out. Even to know one can do nothing.'

She was now standing and soaping herself. He hoped she would not ask him to rub her shoulders. He didn't want to touch that wart, or whatever it was. He didn't want to see it again.

'You've been there, you must know something . . .' he said.

'I know that no man should be so rich that he could afford to buy an island,' she was now sitting and rubbing her toes. 'It happened some sixty years ago. You must have been a young man then. My parents can't have been very much older than you.' She stretched out in the bath and said, 'I'm, tired. I haven't slept for three days.'

'You mustn't fall asleep in your bath,' he said. He handed her some towels and his bathrobe. 'Go straight to bed and I'll bring you something to eat. You need it.'

'Don't be long,' she said. 'I don't want to be alone. What I need is to talk. I want to talk. To talk. Talk, talk, talk.'

Back in the kitchen, he concentrated again on his scrambled eggs on toast and coffee, and yet – for the last few days – whatever he was doing, his ears had kept a constant watchout for the ringing of the telephone bell. It was shortly after the morning when his son had rung to ask those unusual questions: 'Is Lucy there?' 'Is Deborah there?' that he had decided to go to see him and find out what was going on. A burly big man opened the door and asked 'What do you want?'; 'I want to see Mr Adam D'Earth,' Sean said. 'He's not in,' the man announced and asked, 'And who are you?'; 'I am his father. And who are *you*?' The man took from his breast pocket a little card with his photograph, showed it, and put it back. 'I'm guarding the place, sir,' the man said. 'And Lady Lucy, and their daughter Deborah?' Sean asked. 'There's nobody in, sir,' the man said. 'I know I mustn't ask too many questions,' Sean said, 'but is there anything you *can* tell me?' The man took one look at Sean, said, 'If you'll wait a moment, sir,' and turned to the door. When he came back, he said, 'You'll be notified if something has happened, sir.' Sean didn't like it. 'I would prefer somebody to be good enough to let me know that nothing has happened,' he said. 'Perhaps I expressed myself badly,' the man said. 'What I meant was – you'll be telephoned.' Sean still didn't like it. 'Shall I give you my telephone number?' he asked. '*They* have your telephone number, sir,' the man said. 'Are *they* my son's office or his wife's?' he asked. 'No matter, sir. Somebody'll phone you.'

Nobody had. The telephone remained soundless. It was the front doorbell that had rung to let in the Shepherd woman, Miss or Mrs or both, with her strange story of the desert island. 'Bah . . .' he said to himself, putting the scrambled eggs and coffee on a tray.

She was lying in bed, her eyes wide open. At the first moment, as he entered the room, he thought that she had just stopped laughing. But it must have been a spasm of – well, of what? He didn't know. He put the tray on the bed. 'All this must be eaten,' he said, and sat down in the armchair.

'Eggs,' she said. 'I haven't eaten many eggs in my life. Hens were not allowed on the Island. They were considered to be animals. We had to order eggs from Ireland. The children loved them.'

What had she said? He blamed his old age for being so slow. He had to repeat for himself the words he had just heard. 'Hens were considered to be animals?' Either he had misheard it, or . . . But at that very moment the telephone rang. He got up and rushed to the next room.

'Yes?' he said.

'Er . . . is a Mrs Shepherd there?' the voice asked.

'What?!'

'Put her on to me. I want to ask her a few questions.'

'And who are you?'

'A few questions about your son, Mr D'Earth.'

'How is my son?'

'Let me talk to her first, and I'll tell you later.'

'Look here, I didn't . . .' he started (saying to himself, Oh no, I want to talk to her first!) – and then, to his relief, some clicking and clucking noises filled the earpiece. What was it? telephone tapping? crossed lines? and then another voice shouted, 'Get off the line! Get off the line I say!' Was it shouting at him or at the the other chap, the one who was phoning him? He replaced the receiver but picked it up again, at once. The voice was still there, saying, 'It was *The Resurrection*, yes, *Resurrection*, and the gunboat was French, repeat, French!' to which the first voice exclaimed, 'God Almighty . . .' and, abruptly, as if cut off with a knife, dead silence.

Back in his armchair, he said, 'Somebody wanted to talk to you, Mrs Shepherd.'

'Oh no,' she said. 'Please don't let them. Your son told me not to talk to anybody. He told me nobody can help anyway. He said that the things I had seen are State Secrets, and they will arrest me, and silence me, if they think that I know anything. He only let me go so that I'd come and see you and tell you that he loves you and has always loved you and that you were right and that he is sorry.'

'Why should he feel sorry?' he asked.

'I don't know. Perhaps he thought that all that was his fault.'

'What was his fault?'

'Well, the things that happened there.'

'What things?'

'Oh,' she screamed.

He waited a minute, and then he said, 'Well, my dear, you must tell me. You know that you must, don't you?'

'I don't know how to tell it. It is so . . . Oh God . . . I don't know where to start . . .'

'Start from the beginning,' he said.

'I've already told you. At the beginning there was a mad millionaire who bought the Island, built the Big House and the farmhouse, brought in my parents to be caretakers, and jumped out of the window, without telling them what it was all about. And, without knowing what it was all about, my parents lived happily on the Island for nearly thirty-five years, and – after they died – we lived there happily for a further twenty-five years or so, all by ourselves, happily, thinking it would be like that for ever, and then it happened, suddenly, with hardly any warning, the Island became invaded, some strange people crowded into it, and . . . Well, first, those two rude men who landed on the southern tip and upset us all. And the next morning it was *The Resurrection* . . .

'Did you say "*Resurrection*"?' he asked. Was that not the word he had just overheard on the phone?

'Yes,' she said. 'A funny name for a boat. She was painted all white and looked more like a yacht than a cargo boat. Perhaps she was a big yacht. Too big to come near the shore. It was a rowing dinghy that brought them to our little jetty. The Captain and a little black man. The Captain, as soon as I saw him, I fell for him. He reminded me of something I had never seen, if you see what I mean. Or, perhaps, well, I don't know. The only time I was in a theatre was . . . in London, some twenty years ago. But I was so busy with my own thoughts then that I didn't even notice the play. It may be that there was a man like the Captain there, on the stage, or in the audience, I don't know. Anyway, as soon as I saw him, my knees went weak. He was so smart . . . He must have been about fifty . . . Perhaps a year younger. Or older. He was wearing a white captain's hat, a navy blazer, a striped tie, white trousers . . . And he had a smiling face. The other man was much smaller and he was black and he was wearing an evening dress with tails and plenty of decorations, rows of medals, and white rubber-soled canvas shoes. All the same, he looked very dignified because he carried himself so upright. And as we were walking to our farmhouse, the Captain introduced himself. "My name is Captain Plain-Smith, capital *P* and a hyphen, that's to say that's what they call me to my face. Behind my back they call me Captain Pain-in-the-neck, which I rather like, in my own sort of way. And this is Dr Archibald Janson, you write it J-A-N but you pronounce it YAN. No, he's not a doctor of medicine or of divinity. If you ask him, he'll tell you he's a doctor *honoris causa*, which is a

131

posh thing to be. But I'll tell you something in secret. Only don't tell anybody that you know. You see, Dr Janson is actually a dethroned king. Well, not so much a dethroned king as a deposed president of an African republic. So, you see, Dr Janson is to be treated with due respect. In particular, he mustn't be given any money. Royalty doesn't handle money. And he mustn't be allowed to use your boat. Deposed presidents mustn't risk being seasick.''

'I looked at Dr Janson, his face didn't show any reaction, as if he were above that kind of idle talk. And I thought it would be quite an experience to have such a character on our Island. Actually, the Captain said, it wasn't his business to tell us all that about the Doctor. It was a lady, called Lucy, who was in charge, and it was planned that it would be she who comes first with a red carpet and a toothbrush and some clothes for the Doctor, but he, the Captain, was tired of holding *The Resurrection* stationary in the middle of the ocean, as if she were an old puff-puff steam-engine forgotten at the terminal of a branch line. No, he confessed, he was tired of waiting, tired of being *As idle as a painted ship Upon a painted ocean*, so he decided to misread and not query the garbled signal he received, and to come at once, and that was how it happened that *The Resurrection* arrived at the Island the day before, and not (as it was planned in London) the day after the arrival of the lady called Lucy, and the words *As idle as a painted ship Upon a painted ocean* were so beautiful, they couldn't have been the Captain's own words, surely they were the words of a poet and the Captain just quoted them, *As idle as a painted ship Upon a painted ocean*, I didn't mind any more that he, the Captain, would go back to his *Resurrection*, perhaps never to be seen again, if he left with me those beautiful words, a beautiful diamond bracelet of words, *As idle as a painted ship Upon a painted ocean*, I had lived all my life surrounded by the real ocean, and had seen many real ships passing by, but nothing real was so beautiful as those words *As idle as a painted ship Upon a painted ocean*, words I could repeat again and again endlessly and make them sound more and more graspable, I mean more deeply and deeply com-pre-hen-sible, I have always felt like that about words, especially those in books or on the radio, where they are separated from pictures, so that you can enjoy them in their purity; take Herr Braun for instance, he used to come to the Island every two or three years and I can hardly say what he looks like, but I do remember exactly word for word everything he said twenty years ago and seventeen years ago and fifteen years ago and twelve years ago and so on and just a few days ago, because, you know, he also came to the Island, he came the next day, the day the lady called Lucy came with her red carpet and toothbrush, but oh dear, we are not there yet, we are still with Captain Pain-in-the-neck and Dr Janson, we are standing in front of our farmhouse, Gregory and I facing the Captain and the Doctor, our children Louise, Jane and Philip behind us, and old Nemo, old Nemo – nobody knew how old he was by now – old Nemo behind the children, towering above all of us. And now my Gregory thought that he should make a speech; what gave him that idea I don't know, but he took a deep breath and said, "You are welcome, gentlemen. We expected you because we were told you would be coming, but it is unexpected because we weren't told when; we were told, *Details will follow*, but they didn't. Now, more than that, as a matter of fact Herr Braun told me – already twenty years ago! – that you might be coming one day, so you may say that we've been waiting for you for twenty years, and perhaps we should offer you a drink to toast your coming, but we have no drinks on the Island, we may order some to be brought with the next delivery, if you tell us what kind of drinks you drink."

' "Hear! Hear!" Captain Plain-Smith nodded in approval.

' "This is a peaceful island," Gregory continued, "We have *narcissus poeticus* in spring, our bees produce honey both for themselves and for us in summer, we have apples and pears in autumn, and our winters are mild and friendly. We hardly ever see anybody and are not used to speaking to people. We are a quiet little island, and if you see us so disturbed today, it is quite exceptional, and it is not because of your visit, which is most welcome, no, it is those two rude men who arrived here yesterday, and are still here, it is their presence that we find so disturbing." My poor Gregory was out of breath now, but he soldiered on. "As you were making your way here, gentlemen, you must have noticed the strange vessel anchored off the southern tip of the island. It was from her that the flat-bottomed boat came yesterday with those two men and some apparatuses. Seeing them coming, I walked to the southern tip to greet them politely and ask what they wanted, but before I had time to say a word, they asked *me* what *I* was doing here! Imagine! I, who was born here, here where my mother and father and Matilda are buried, here, where my children were born. What was I doing here, they asked!"

'After that, as he stopped for a moment, our son Philip piped up, "They've come to look for where to dump their radioactive waste."

'Then Gregory said, "You may be right, son, or else you may be wrong, I cannot know. But if you are right . . ."

'Then I screamed.

'Then Jane screamed, "Mummy!"

'Then Louise said, "They wouldn't dare to dump their radio-active dirt in Swiss soil."

'Then Captain Plain-Smith asked, "Why did you say *Swiss* soil, Miss?"

'Then Louise said, "Well, Herr Braun is Swiss, isn't he? And so was Herr Fischer before him, and that other Herr before Herr Fischer."

'Then the Captain said, "But you are English, Miss, are you not?"

'Then Louise said, "I suppose we are."

134

'Then Jane said, "I was at school in Ireland."

'Then Philip said, "We'll fight them. The dashing Swiss Guard will help us to fight them!"

'Then Jane said, "The Swiss Guard isn't Swiss, you silly. The Swiss Guard is in the Vatican, guarding the Pope."

'Then Philip cried, "So why is it called Swiss?"

'Then Jane said, "That's history."

'Then Philip said, "My foot!"

'Then I said, "Children . . . Children . . ."

'And then Dr Janson moved his little finger. I mean it literally. You see, all the time we were talking and shouting, he had been standing there, as stiff as a poker, his arms folded over his decorated chest, and now he lifted the little finger of his right hand, the finger was brown on the finger-nail side and sort of pinkish on the palm side, and he lifted it and it alone was sticking up, and we all stopped talking and shouting and we looked at Dr Janson's little finger, in silence, waiting to see what was going to happen, and Dr Janson turned his head just a little, just enough to look at Gregory, and he said, "Mr Governor, sir," that's what he said, and it was as if a new chapter of the History of the Island had opened, suddenly. We knew that the Americans say "Mr President, sir", and the MPs in the House of Commons say "Mr Speaker, sir", but nobody had ever before called Gregory "Mr Governor, sir", some fishermen would call him "Governor", yes, but it was not the same, and the very moment Dr Janson said "Mr Governor, sir", our children saw their father in a new light, and he saw himself in a new light, because these three magic words "Mr Governor, sir" had changed the very colour of the Island's sunlight, and we knew that from then on everything would look different, and we hung upon Dr Janson's lips, and he paused for a moment and then said, "Will you be so good as to guide us to the place where the two intruders are now?" – and it was a question, and it sounded like a question, very politely put, courteously, but we all knew that it was an order,

135

and we all knew that even if Gregory was now "Mr Governor, sir", it was Dr Janson who was the King of the Island, or a Viceroy.

'And so, without a word, Gregory turned south and started walking, and we all followed, Gregory and Dr Janson, then I and the Captain, then Philip, then the two girls, and Nemo at the end of the procession. Half-way there, we could already see the top of the bright yellow tent the two men had pitched at the very tip of the island. As we came nearer, they were standing there, waiting for us. Two men in their twenties. In some sort of outfit that could have been a military fatigue dress or perhaps a hippie sort of style. But Dr Janson didn't even look at them. He turned to Captain Pain-in-the-neck and said, "Captain, ask these people to show you their papers."

'And the Captain said, "Your papers, please."

'And one of the men said, "What papers?"

'And the Captain said, "Your permission to land on the Island."

'And the man said, "We were told that this is a desert island. Nobody lives here."

'And the Captain said, "Who told you that?"

'And the other man said, "Take it easy, old man, we're here on duty, same as yourself."

'And the Captain said, "Prove it."

'And it went on like that, but then Dr Janson cut it short. He looked at his wristwatch (he still had his watch, I'm telling you that because that Patek gold watch was part of the bargain when – as I learned later – he was sold by the French computer salesmen to the British Intelligence for seventy-eight bottles of Scotch whisky) and so, as I said, he looked at his wristwatch and said, "Captain, give them one hour to clear off."

'And so the Captain said, "You heard it. You have one hour to clear off."

'And they looked rather sheepish; well, they were just two, but we were five men – Dr Janson, the Captain, Gregory,

Nemo, and Philip quite ready to start a fight, and three women – Louise, Jane, and myself, and of course they couldn't know how many men there were aboard *The Resurrection*. On the other hand, we didn't know how many there were aboard their ship anchored not so very far away. All the same, we won and they lost. And so we were now returning in a spirit of jubilation. Specially Philip, looking with admiration now at the Doctor now at the Captain, mimicking now the one now the other, and the girls, flashing glances at them, the girls had never seen anything like it, not in real life, not on the Island; actually, neither had I, but I did have my misgivings, and so I was sure did Gregory, because as we started to come back one of the two men said, "When a signal about all this reaches the high-ups in London, it will be your funeral", that's what he said at the end, well, of course, he said it in defiance, but all the same I knew there must have been more to it, but what it was I didn't know at the time, and it's only now that I see what it was, it was that we there on the Island were squeezed between two official secrets which didn't know about each other, the top secret of your son Adam, and the top secret of his wife Lucy. Well, it might have been that your son and his wife had no private secrets, it may be that in bed they told each other everything private about themselves, that I don't know. But what I do know is that what his official secret was he kept to himself and from her, and what her official secret was she kept to herself and from him, otherwise he would have known where she was going, she would have told him that Hobson's Island is not a bit of dead rock, as it was marked on the Admiralty charts, and he would have to find some other place for whatever were those clever things he planned to do. I didn't know all that at the time, neither did Gregory, but we knew it wasn't the end of our troubles and, all the same, as I said, we were jubilant, and, as we walked, the south wind was pushing forward, making us half-run half-fight with it joyfully, that's to say, all of us except Dr Janson, no wind would dare to disturb him, to interfere with the erect carriage of his body; he walked at a steady pace, so dignified, stately, and it wasn't at all funny when he stumbled over the roots of some prickly brambles and nearly fell. Gregory helped him, and we went on, and when we were passing the Big House, Dr Janson said, 'I'll have my rooms on the first floor, on the corner, with windows giving on to the east and north.' That was typical of him. He was on the Island for the first time, and seemed to know everything about it, he had never seen the Big House before, and he knew which rooms he wanted to have. And then he said, "I shall not dine with you tonight," and he said it before it even occurred to us to ask him. And he excused himself, he said, "Captain Plain-Smith has invited me to my last supper aboard *The Resurrection*, a farewell dinner party." I already knew that my *painted ship Upon a painted ocean* would leave us before midnight, the ship would go, Pain-in-the-neck would go, still, – those beautiful words would stay with me for ever; for ever, that's what I thought; and then Dr Janson said, "I shall be back in my rooms at twenty-two hours exactly but there will be no need to wait for me. I will find my way. I suppose doors are not locked and there is no need for keys on the Island, am I right?" Even the Captain looked at Dr Janson with what I thought was a mixture of surprise, curiosity and admiration. And while I calculated which o'clock twenty-two hours was, Dr Janson said, "I shall have breakfast in my rooms. Perhaps Mademoiselle Louise will be good enough to bring it on a tray."

'Now Louise blushed, Jane giggled, and Philip clenched his two fists tightly. And I didn't know if he did that because he thought that it was he who should have the honour of carrying the tray, or because he thought that his sister was in danger and he must be ready to defend her. Anyway, I was afraid the boy might do something silly, so I said quickly, "What would you like for breakfast, Dr Janson?"

'And he said, "Exactly the same that you have."

'And I said, "Our breakfasts are mostly vegetarian, Dr Janson."

'And he said, "That suits me perfectly well, Mrs Shepherd."

'And that was that. I prepared the rooms on the first floor of the Big House, and I told myself I must remember to warn Louise not to stay longer than necessary when she took the breakfast tray tomorrow morning to Dr Janson, and to remember to watch Philip, but the next morning, still before breakfast time, a helicopter landed on the north half of the island, bringing Lady Lucy, her daughter Deborah, and Deborah's young friend John; and then a sailing boat came with two young French people Pierrot and Marie-Claire, and an Italian lady called Zuppa and her friend a Dr Goldfinger; and in the afternoon a fishing boat from Ireland brought Herr Braun; and as if that wasn't enough, a speedboat disembarked a young American called Hobson, and – for the first time in the history of the world – our little island became as over-crowded as Piccadilly Circus which I saw twenty years ago when I went to a theatre in London. So now you are in the picture, Mr D'Earth,' she said.

'Yes . . .' he said. And, after a long while, he added 'Go on . . . please . . .'

But she covered her head with the blanket and he heard her choking, but he could have sworn that she was choking with laughter.

## SIX

## *The Salt of the Earth*

'You said I needed a drink, Mr D'Earth. I think I would like one now,' she said.

But now he wasn't sure if she should, and he said, 'Are you sure that you should?'

'Yes please,' she said. 'It will help me to talk.'

And then she sniffed at the little brandy he gave her, she sniffed it in as if it were sea air. Then she sighed. Then she looked at him and said, 'May I have my suitcase, please.'

He fetched her suitcase, put it beside the bed, but she didn't open it.

'You said the Island became overcrowded,' he tried to prompt her. 'So many people, you said. On the same day, you said. Lucy and Deborah, and all the others. But you didn't mention Adam. Was he not there?'

'No,' she said.

And she paused.

And he regretted that he had asked. She had to tell it in her own way. So he didn't ask any more questions. And she said 'A little island is a living thing. When your ear hears music, your foot, there, far away, on the other end of your body, beats out the rhythm. When your big toe is hurt, the muscles of your face wince. When your eye sees something beautiful, your whole body becomes tense. It is the same with the little Island. On whichever bit of the Island anything happened, the whole Island was aware of it, the whole Island knew. And so did I. I always knew where Gregory was coming from, what Nemo was doing, where Philip was going to, what Jane was reading, what Louise was thinking, I just knew. And when the strangers came, I just knew the same about them, without spying or eavesdropping, I knew because I was part of my little Island and I knew what the Island knew. And because I was a part of it, they, the strangers, the visitors, they could not isolate me from the rest of the Island, and so it was as if I were like one of the anonymous trees – invisible though not transparent, or like the spaces between the trees – visible but transparent. And so . . . "Oh, you are here, I didn't notice you," Lady Lucy would say, going up the stairs to the top floor where all those electronic gadgets were stored under the roof, still, since the beginning of the war; or *"Je vous demande pardon, Madame,"* Pierrot would say, brushing past me, as he ran to the top floor. So he followed Lady Lucy, but I didn't follow him. I went down and stood in front of the front door, and I looked to the right and saw Dr Janson coming towards me and exclaiming, "I say I say!" But I saw that he wasn't addressing me. So I looked to my left, and there were that Italian lady, Princess Zuppa and her friend. And they and Dr Janson stopped just in front of me, facing each other, but to me they paid no attention at all. I was an invisible woman there. So, as I said, Dr Janson exclaimed, "I say I say! What are you doing here?! You, of all people! Here, of all places!"

'To which Princess Zuppa said, "Dear brother, will it surprise you if I tell you that I came here especially to see you?"

'And this, I must say, sounded more true. Because, you see, Mr D'Earth, when they arrived on their powerful little boat that pretended to be a sailing boat and displayed a little French Tricolour, they were a bit confused, Pierrot and Marie-Claire, and Princess Zuppa and Dr Goldfinger, at first they said they had lost their bearings, then Pierrot said that the Princess had hired him because she wanted to see the smallest island on this side of the Atlantic, to which Gregory said Hobson's Island is not the smallest, there are many much smaller ones among the Scilly Islands, to which Pierrot said, "Yes, but they are British," to which Gregory said, "So is Hobson's Island"; to which Pierrot said, "It all depends. Ethnographically it might be British, if you who live here are British. But geologically it is French"; to which Gregory said, "Nonsense. It is twice as far from here to France as it is to Cornwall"; to which Marie-Claire said, "*Bien sûr, mais* if you look at the bottom of the sea, *le fond de la mer*, you'll see the rift, the dividing line between the Scilly Isles which still belong to the Caledonian folding, and your Hobson's Island which is Hercynian, and, during the ice age, the Riss period, they, the Scillies, were under the sheet of ice, while Hobson's Island, like the rest of France, was not and the proof is that on the intrusive rocks of your Scilly Isles no trees grow, but here there are these beautiful trees, here on Hobson's Island, just the same as in France"; to which I said, "Please come ashore and stretch your legs and I'll give you a cup of coffee"; to which they said, "You are *bien gentille, Madame*," and they came to the farmhouse and brought a bottle of Pernod with them; and at that time Dr Janson was in his rooms brushing his teeth with the toothbrush Lady Lucy had brought him, and shaving with the shaving kit Lady Lucy had brought him, and putting on the tweeds Lady Lucy had brought him, and so he didn't see the new arrivals, and, as I said, it was only now that he saw them and exclaimed, "I say I say! What are you doing here?! You, of all people! Here, of all places!" To which, as I have already said, Princess Zuppa said, "Dear brother, will it surprise you if I tell you that I came here especially to see you?"

'And Dr Janson looked at her searchingly, and said, "Are you armed?"

'And Princess Zuppa said, "No, I'm not."

'And he said, "Show me your handbag, please," and he added quickly, "No, don't open it."

'And she handed him her handbag, and he glanced into it,

and gave it back to her. Then he turned to Dr Goldfinger and said, "And you, sir, are you armed?"

'And Dr Goldfinger put his hands up, grinned, and mocked his own gesture. "Search me," he said, not thinking, surely, that Dr Janson would go beyond a joke.

'But he did. He patted Dr Goldfinger's pockets, then he stepped back and said, "In my position, one cannot be too careful."

'But she said, "We are not your enemies, brother."

'And he said, "Ha ha. You don't know what you are saying, sister. The fact is that my enemies are my friends, and my friends are my enemies. I'm all on the side of the revolutionaries who have dethroned me. I forced them to do so. It is the old patriotic prigs, who supported me, that I am against. And so the British are doubly puzzled. First, they haven't made up their minds whom to back – the new regime or the old regime. Second: the new regime will not have me, and the old one – I don't want to lead. And so it seems that I'm stuck here for good." He winked at Princess Zuppa and, in a different tone of voice, asked, "Tell me, sister, the real reason. What was it that made you come here to see me?"

'She thought for a moment and then said, "A sort of sentimental curiosity."

'Now he asked very quickly, "You came here by boat, of course . . ."

'And she said, "Yes."

'And he said, "So you could smuggle me out of here?"

'And she said, "Perhaps I could, I don't know. But I would not advise you to try."

'And he said, "Why not?"

'And she said, "Well, *entre nous*, the young couple that sailed us here are in the French secret service. They would deliver you to their bosses, and for you it would be out of the frying-pan into the fire."

'But he said, "I must find my way to Switzerland. Once I'm there, money is no problem. They will not do it for money?"

'She said, "They won't."

'He said, "Well, forget it."

'And then Dr Goldfinger said, "You said, sir, you forced the revolutionaries to dethrone you. Why did you do that, sir, if I may ask?"

'To which Dr Janson replied, "I did it for the sake of Bukumla. So that they could build their Jerusalem as they desired it."

'To which Dr Goldfinger said, "But you were the ruler, sir. Could you not do it yourself?"

'To which Dr Janson said, "No, sir. Those things cannot be done from above. They have to be done from below."

'To which Dr Goldfinger said, "Even at the price of bloodshed?"

'To which Dr Janson said, "Do you know of a State, any kind of State, monarchy or republic, created by peaceful means?"

'To which Dr Goldfinger said, "But is a State the only structure in which a civilized life can exist? Do we need all those innumerable States?"

'To which Dr Janson said, "Some people don't need States, and some people do. And that's that. The same as with God. Some people don't need God, and some do. And that's that. Some people don't need to believe, and some do. And that's that."

'To which Princess Zuppa said, "God is not the only thing one can believe in."

'To which Dr Janson said, "What else is there to believe in?"

'To which Princess Zuppa said, "One can believe in Decency."

'And then they didn't say a word for a long time. And something made me think again of those beautiful words which I had collected from Captain Pain-in-the-neck, *As idle as a painted ship Upon a painted ocean*, and now I had been given a gift of five more words which were spreading into every part of me: *One can believe in Decency*; now, the Captain's words were *poetry*, and Princess Zuppa's words were *prose*, and poetry may sound true even if it isn't true, but prose, even if true, does not always sound true, and so I thought: Could Princess Zuppa's prose be made into poetry, so that it would not only *be* true but also *sound* true, and I asked myself, Who could do that? and I knew the answer: that girl who came by helicopter with Lady Lucy, Deborah; yes, I knew she could do that, I knew, because as soon as the helicopter landed and the door slid open, she jumped out and ran to the edge of the shore and started talking to the Ocean, addressing it as if it were a woman, Hail holy Ocean, the Whore of Whores, hail our life, our sweetness and our hope! To thee we cry, poor banished children of Eve, to thee do we send up our sighs, we, the emotional arseholes, mourning and weeping in this womb of tears, no – she wasn't singing, she was just saying words, and I thought that if she could say such words as whores and arseholes and wombs so that they sounded poetic, then she could transform Princess Zuppa's prose into Captain Pain-in-the-neck's poetry, but that was just a thought, something that passes through one's mind and goes, because what really thought itself there in my mind, all the time, was what to do with Louise, my daughter; no, she didn't take the breakfast tray to Dr Janson after all, the helicopter had landed just before breakfast time and all our plans had turned topsy turvy: Dr Janson had breakfast with Lady Lucy, so Philip grinned from ear to ear, but Louise was disappointed and I thought more and more about her, she was already eighteen and she had hardly seen any men, and now there were so many of them on the island, there was Dr Goldfinger, he was very very old; and there was Dr Janson, he must have been more than twice her age; but then there was that French boy Pierrot, with the girl called Marie-Claire; and John, the friend of Deborah; and the helicopter pilot, but he left as soon as they unloaded. No, I didn't ask myself such questions about Jane, who was only one year younger. But Louise was different. Louise wanted to see the world. Louise wanted to experience the world. I don't say she wanted to leave the Island. No, she wanted to bring the world to the Island and experience it there. When Herr Braun, on his visit two years ago, saw Louise and Nemo swimming in the sea naked, her eyes sparkling, he took Gregory and me aside and asked if we were sure that it was all right, that it was safe, but we all of us used to swim naked, and Louise's eyes were always sparkling, and I was sure it was all right, because I knew about Nemo, I knew that Nemo was in love with our mother. No, I don't mean that he used to make love to her, no, certainly not, at least not when she was alive, because when she died we had a photograph of her, taken before she married our father, a postcard size picture of her playing tennis in shorts and a T-shirt, and when she died we saw that he wanted to have it and we gave it to him, and I knew that looking at it helped him when he had to rid himself of some of his semen, when its tide was up, well, that's, as you said, Mr D'Earth, the Mystery of the Body or the Chemistry of the Body or both, so now I have three precious strings of words in my collection: *As idle as a painted ship Upon a painted ocean*, and *One can believe in Decency*, yes, not in "Concern for others", not in "Duty", not in "Reciprocity", but in "Decency", and *The Mystery of the Body or the Chemistry of the Body or both*, and it so happened once that I thought of helping him, Nemo, to do what he was doing, but then I was afraid I might grow to like it, and, as he was in need of it regularly once a week, the thing would complicate our life on the Island, so I did not, and when the helicopter landed, just before breakfast, and they unloaded, there was there among other things a red carpet, but they didn't need it any more, first – because it was too late for greeting Dr Janson as he was already on the Island, and then – he wasn't to be a VIP after all, he was just a Dr Janson now, so Lady Lucy gave the carpet to us, but we didn't have anywhere to put it, so we gave it to Nemo, and Nemo liked it, but he didn't lay it on the floor, he hung it on the wall by his bed, and pinned the photograph of mother in the centre of it, and as I was having all those thoughts, Dr Janson broke the silence, and said, "My God, we are three grown people here (I was there all the time, but he only counted Princess Zuppa, Dr Goldfinger, and himself) and we are talking like students in a café in the Latin Quarter! Now, listen, I've just been given a case of claret by Lady Lucy, my official guardian angel. Shall we go to my rooms and sample it?"

'And so they went round the corner to the other door, leading to Dr Janson's rooms, and I went upstairs, to the top floor, to see what Lady Lucy and Pierrot were doing there. It was my Island. I should know what was going on. And something was going on.

'They were sitting side by side behind a long table which I used to dust from time to time, the table and all those old-fashioned radio receivers and transmitters and aerials of many different shapes. They were wearing headphones but they were not listening. The headphones were hanging round their necks like doctors' stethoscopes. Pads of writing paper were placed neatly in front of them and the black remains of burnt papers filled the ashtrays. As I came in, I heard her saying, "You are a great cynic, my dear Pierrot, are you not?"

'And Pierrot answered, "*Mais . . . chère Madame*, you must admit that it is from our own *populace* that we hide things, not from our potential enemies."

'And Lady Lucy said, "I don't admit anything of the sort. Well, not wholly."

'And Pierrot went on, "From our potential enemies, we only hide little things. The big, important things we insist on showing to their agents, so that they would know that we are not bluffing, that our tanks are not made of *papier mâché* and our missiles are not filled with *merde*."

'To which she said, "You are a naughty boy, my dear Pierrot."

'But Pierrot insisted, "You know, and I know, Madame, that *we* are the salt of the earth. Why don't we share our intelligence then? If I tell you what I have just signalled, will you tell me what you have?"

'She lit a cigarette and said, "You tell first, and then we'll see."

'And he said, "I told them that there is a sinister-looking ship anchored off the south end. Needing an expert examination."

'And she said, "Oh, is there?" And then she added, "I said there is a couple of innocent-looking French agents here, a boy called Pierrot and a girl who pretends to be his wife."

'And he said, "Why did you say *pretend*, Madame?"

'She didn't answer. She just looked at him, and he blushed. But then I heard something they didn't. I ran to the window. Two new arrivals: an Irish coaster already mooring by our little jetty, and an English speedboat just coming. I rushed down and they followed me. "Seems like open day here," Lady Lucy said.

•

'The Irish coaster had brought Herr Braun, as I might have guessed. He used to come from Switzerland via Dublin. We thought he had some business, or perhaps some friends, there, but he never told us, and we didn't ask. I greeted him, and I said, "As you see, Herr Braun, your prediction of twenty years ago is being fulfilled," and I introduced him to Lady Lucy and to Pierrot. They said, "How do you do . . .", they said,"M'sieur . . .", they said, "Madame . . .", they said "Enchanté . . .", they shook hands, and then Herr Braun pointed to the speedboat and asked, "And that . . . ?"

' "I have no idea," I said.

148

'The speedboat was aiming at a point on the other side of the jetty, where our children were standing, looking at her with admiration. At her, and at a tall young man with a suitcase standing on the fore deck. Before she even touched dry land, the young man with the suitcase jumped, and the boat immediately backed, turned round, and rushed north by east. "Hi!" the young man said.

'The girls smiled, and Philip, trying to copy the man's voice, said, "Hi!"

'The man pointed to the Big House and said, "Is *that* the hotel?"

'Philip looked puzzled. "No, it isn't," he said.

'The man took a dollar bill from his wallet and gave it to Philip. "Will you show me the way to a hotel, boy?"

'Philip looked at the dollar bill and didn't know what it was. So he said smartly, "And what am I expected to do with this?"

' "You can go to a shop, boy, and buy yourself a Pepsi, or bubble-gum, or comics. How can I know what you might want?"

' "There are no shops here," Philip said.

'The man whistled.

' "and there are no hotels either," Philip said.

'The man snatched his dollar bill out of the boy's hand, turned, came to us, and said, "The boy there is pulling my leg. Tells me there are no hotels on the island."

' "The boy was telling the truth," I told him. "There are no hotels here, or anything of the sort."

'He didn't say it at once. He waited a moment, and only then said rather bitterly, "My name is Hobson, this is my grandfather's island, and there isn't a bed on it for me to spend the night."

'Pierrot murmured, "*Ça, par exemple . . .*"

'Lady Lucy said under her breath, "Hobson . . . ?"

'But Herr Braun's address was loud and clear. "Welcome to the Island, I'm sure," he said. And, pointing at me, he went on, "This is Mrs Shepherd, our hostess. I'm sure Mrs Shepherd will be glad to put you up. Perhaps in the room next to mine? Will that be all right, Mrs Shepherd?"

'Though Herr Braun used to come only once every two or three years, and even then he didn't always stay overnight, there was one room in the Big House where he kept a few personal things, his *nécessaire de toilette* et cetera, as he called it. "Yes, of course, Herr Braun," I said.

'And then Herr Braun said, "Let me introduce myself, Mr Hobson. My name is Herr Braun."

'And Mr Hobson asked, "Hermann Braun?"

'And Herr Braun explained, "No, not Hermann. *Herr*, Herr Braun, you can call me Mr Braun, if you'd rather."

'And Mr Hobson repeated, "Oh, Herr Braun. Are you German?"

'To which Herr Braun answered, "No, I am not German. I am Swiss."

'Mr Hobson's eyes looked as if something in his brain was doing its homework. "Are you a banker, Herr Braun?" he asked.

' "Let's say I'm a bank's lawyer," Herr Braun said.

' "You don't say . . . Are you here on business or for pleasure?"

' "Business is my pleasure, Mr Hobson," Herr Braun said.

' "Good. Maybe we could do some business together . . . Hey! Where are you going, you there . . . ?!" he shouted. He was shouting at Pierrot who had taken his suitcase and was going off with it.

' "I'm taking it to your room," Pierrot said.

' "I'm strong enough to carry it myself, thank you," Mr Hobson said, ready to go after him.

'But at that moment we seemed to have become surrounded: the children came from the other side of the jetty; Dr Janson, Princess Zuppa and Dr Goldfinger from the Big House; Gregory and Nemo from the farmhouse; Deborah and her friend John were running towards us from the other side of the Island. And then Pierrot appeared again, saying, "Your suitcase is in your room, Mr Hobson."

'Perhaps I was the only one who noticed that at that moment everybody was there, that's to say: everybody, except Marie-Claire. When, a few minutes later, I went to the room next to Herr Braun's room, I mean the room which I had to make ready for Mr Hobson, I found Marie-Claire there, sitting on the suitcase. *"Pierrot m'a dit de vous donner un coup de main,"* she said. I didn't know the expression, but she looked so sweet that I assumed Pierrot had *not* asked her to box me.

## SEVEN

## Double Helix of Love, Hate and Decency

'What am I doing here, Mr D'Earth, in your bathrobe, in your bed, in this strange town? Your bathrobe is very soft and warm, Mr D'Earth, and it smells nicely of *l'eau de Cologne* and of you. And now it will smell also of me, and I'm smelling already of my baby. Oh, it is still months and months . . . to carry it in my belly, but it has already kicked me. It. Will it be a boy or a girl? No, don't worry, Mr D'Earth, it will not be born here, in your bed. No. Oh, here or anywhere else, a boy or a girl, I hope it will scream, I hope it will scream as it is born, I hope it will not laugh. Because, if it laughs as it is born, it will mean that it is dead. That's how it is, Mr D'Earth. That's how it is.

'I didn't know that it was like that, at the time, and when I spoke to Princess Zuppa, I told her "Princess Zuppa, you said that some people believe in God, but you believe in Decency," and she said "Yes, Mrs Shepherd, what about it?" and I said, "But Decency didn't create the world, did it?" and she said, "No, but I'm not interested in that, it's for the physicists to find out how it is that those big balls of stone orbit around each other. Still, you can say that it was Decency that created us, people. Without Decency, mothers and fathers would have eaten their children as soon as the children were born, and that would have been the end even before the beginning." I didn't know whether Princess Zuppa had any children, but I had, and I was again with child, so I said, "But what you are saying, Princess Zuppa, is not Decency. What you are saying is love, isn't it?" And she said, "Oh no, Mrs

152

Shepherd. Beware of love. Love is cruel, and decency is gentle. Love is ugly, and decency is beautiful. Love is easy and decency is difficult. Love creates hate. Imagine that you had fallen in love with me, Mrs Shepherd, immediately you would start to hate Dr Goldfinger." That was strange, what she said. But the next thing she said was still stranger. Because, as I then asked, "You said, Princess Zuppa, that love creates hate. But what does decency create?" – she answered, "Alas, Mrs Shepherd, decency creates love, and that's our human vicious circle."

'She was beautiful, and she was white. "If it embarrasses you to have a black brother, you may call me Archie. My name is now Dr Archibald Janson," Dr Janson said. And then he added, "Though you are probably above such things." She laughed and said, "Of course I am above such things. And you are not. When I wrote to tell you that our father had died, your Chancellery, The Chancellery of the Republic of Bukumla, answered: As the name of General Jan Pięść is not known to His Excellency, it is suggested that your communication might peradventure have been directed to the wrong addressee." And he said, "Come now, be fair, you know very well that the President of Bukumla could not afford to have a white father. What the hell?! He didn't take much care of us, did he? He made love to my mother, he made love to your mother, that was his war effort, I suppose. But all that is ancient history, sister. What interests me now is something about that Swiss Herr Braun. He looks to me as if he owned the Island. He looks to me as if I could do business with him. Do you think, sister . . . ?" he didn't finish his sentence. "I don't know, but I wish you luck," she answered.

'She was beautiful and she was rich. I think it was she who was rich, not Dr Goldfinger. Dr Goldfinger wanted to talk to me. Dr Goldfinger wanted me to tell him what our life on this "lovely island" was like. Actually, it was *he* who was telling me things. Things like: survival in extreme isolation. He said

153

it was interesting because of nuclear war. There used to be, he said, some mutineers concealed for seventeen years on Pitcairn Island, then there was a woman all alone for eighteen years on San Nicolas Island, and then there were Japanese soldiers forgotten for decades on Pacific islands, and so on, but I said, "That has nothing to do with us, Dr Goldfinger, we are a family, we are not isolated, what we can't produce ourselves we have delivered to us about twice a month, we have a big library in the Big House, we have the radio, if we want to we can take a boat and go wherever we want to, but we don't particularly want to – what for? – the very thought of finding myself in Piccadilly Circus, which I saw just once, frightens me, what about all those new machines that give workers the push, three million unemployed, they say, – and why *do* you call them *unemployed*, Dr Goldfinger? When Princess Zuppa gets money that the machines have earned for her, you don't call her *unemployed*, so why, Dr Goldfinger, when those three million people get unemployment benefit money that the machines have earned for them why don't you call them *the three million aristocrats* instead of *the three million unemployed*?" That's what I said, and he laughed, and he said, "There's a deeper meaning in what you've just said, Mrs Shepherd," and I said, "I know there's a deeper meaning in it, Dr Goldfinger, and there's a deeper meaning also in my telling you now that this island is a civilized island because we don't have any of the so many things we do not need." He seemed to agree, in principle, but then he said, "I am a medical man, Mrs Shepherd, and I wonder . . . What do you do when you need a doctor?" He was right. So I said, "You are right, Dr Goldfinger; fortunately the Island herself keeps us fit. And, when the time comes, helps us to die." And then I said, "I did kidnap a doctor once and bring him here to see Mother. He looked at her and said just one word: '*hospital*'. But we didn't want him to prolong her agony. We wanted him to make it easier for her to leave us. He didn't understand

and asked to be taken back home." As I told him that, Dr Goldfinger looked straight into my eyes and said, "Dear Mrs Shepherd, I think that I would have done the same as your doctor. But I understand both him and you." To which I said, "So do I. It seems that God is the only Person that does not." To which he said, "It seems that here on your island, you don't need both a Doctor of Medicine and a Doctor of Divinity." To which I said, "Well, Dr Goldfinger, I must admit that it isn't exactly so. When I was with my first child, Gregory took me to Ireland, to a maternity hospital. So, you see, Louise was born there. And baptized there . . ." and I said quickly, "If you will excuse me, Dr Goldfinger, I must go now."

'And you see, Mr D'Earth, I said so quickly "I must go now" because as soon as I said the words "maternity hospital" something in my brain said, "Oh yes, that's it!" and I went to look for Herr Braun, because – you see, Mr D'Earth – my ear is very good, and when I said "maternity hospital" I at once understood what those words reminded me of, they reminded me of the sounds I heard during the night, when the sea was calm, the sounds brought by the soft breeze from that sinister ship anchored off the south tip of the island – you see, Mr D'Earth – when I was in that maternity hospital, eighteen years ago it was, there I also heard such sounds during the night, they were the sounds of some dozens of little babies' voices, and the sounds coming from the boat the other night were sort of similar sounds, that's why my mind said to me "Oh, yes, that's it", though it wasn't *it* exactly, it was not the babies' sounds, no, definitely not, not of babies, but what it was the sound of, I, at the time, didn't know, all I knew, at the time, was the thought that because of all that excitement, I mean all those people coming to the Island, we had forgotten about the Ship, forgotten about the Menace of the Ship, and so I thought it was most urgent to tell Herr Braun about it, because – you see, Mr D'Earth – Gregory might have been "Mr Governor, sir", Dr Janson might have been a "viceroy or whatever", Lady Lucy might have been "British Intelligence", but it was Herr Braun, obviously, he, Herr Braun, who was the man to talk to, so I looked for Herr Braun to tell him about the Menace of the Ship, but when I found him, he was talking to Dr Janson, who, I guess, wanted to know how he could get to his money in Switzerland, and when I tried again, he, Herr Braun I mean, was busy in conversation with that young American, Mr Hobson, and I know it must have been something serious because they went to Herr Braun's room and stayed there for hours and hours and I didn't see Herr Braun again until the middle of the night.

'Now, dear Mr D'Earth, the middle of the night on the Island is perhaps not the same as the middle of the night here, in London. Nights disembark on the Island as soon as the sun sinks in the sea somewhere beyond the horizon. Then we switch on our little electric light bulbs, hoping that the old windmills have managed to charge the batteries, especially now, with so many people in the Big House.

'And so, dear Mr D'Earth, it was the middle of our Hobson's Island night, the children were already in their rooms, fast asleep, Gregory and I, we had had a long talk and were preparing to go to bed when the door opened and Herr Braun came in. At first, we thought he had come to discuss what to do with all those people, are we going to treat them as guests, or paying guests, or what? But no, we didn't need to think about such things, he said, he and Lady Lucy would sort the muddle out, and he, Herr Braun, had come at such an unusual hour for a quite different reason. Before he started saying what the reason was, I wanted to tell him about the Menace of the Ship, but, clumsily, I started from the wrong end, I started telling him about Lady Lucy and the French boy Pierrot, how they were sitting there in the attic, under the roof, with all those old wireless sets around them, and "And then," I said, "Pierrot said to Lady Lucy 'Why don't we share our intelligence? You know, and I know, Madame, that we are the salt of the earth'," and as I said that, Herr Braun snorted "Hmm . . . two *of those happy souls / Which are the salt of the earth, and without whom / This world would smell like what it is – a tomb*," and I knew he was just quoting or misquoting some poet, as he often used to, but I hated the quotation, no, I wouldn't have it in my collection of words, and when my mind was just revolting against it, I, for a moment, forgot all about the Menace of the Ship, and before it came back to me that I wanted to tell Herr Braun about it, he said very sternly, I mean very seriously, "Listen, my children," (he pronounced "dren" in "children" as if it were spelled like "dern" in "Kindern") "Listen, my children," he said, "what I'm going to tell you is of very great importance, very great importance indeed. I'm going to tell you the whole story, from the very beginning."

'And so, you see, Mr D'Earth, it is as I told you before – do you remember? Herr Braun's story also starts from the same beginning: At the beginning was that mad American millionaire, a Mr Hobson, who some sixty years ago bought the Island, built the Big House and the farmhouse, brought in my parents to be caretakers, and jumped out of the window without telling them what it was all about. "This is a strange story, my children," Herr Braun said. "You see, that Mr Hobson, you know, he bought the Island, but, in a way, he didn't want it for himself; on the other hand, yes he did want it for himself most desperately. You may well ask, How's that? Well, let me tell you what he did and you'll see why he did it. It was a year or two before his death. He came to Switzerland with his lawyer and they said, We want to create a Trust. Expressly for the Island and a big sum of money for its upkeep. They did. And so the Island was no longer his property. It was a Trust. For the benefit of . . . Now, that was the curious thing about it. According to the deed of covenant, it was for the trustees to say who was to be the beneficiary. All that happened more than half a century ago. And yet the trustees

157

haven't yet done anything about it. You may well ask, Why? Well, children, you must know that every single thing in this world has many causes. One of the causes why the trustees haven't yet declared who is going to be the beneficiary is the simple fact that they haven't yet found one. And they haven't found one, because they were not in a hurry. And they weren't in a hurry because of many causes, of which you, children, are one."

'That's what he said, Mr D'Earth, and the way he said it, it took us a bit by surprise. He said it in a sweet soft way, as if he really liked us, you know what I mean, well, yes, you know, we knew all the time that he liked us, but not exactly in that, you know, sort of way. Even his calling us "Children" was . . . well, you see, when he first came to see us, and it was twenty years ago, he must have been just under forty, so he would be just under sixty now, and so his calling us "Children" in that soft way was, you know, sort of touching.

'And so, you see, Mr D'Earth, he said that it was because they, the trustees, liked us. And not only the trustees, of whom he was one, but some other people as well, there, in Switzerland, they, as he said, were *interested* in us, they called us "The English Family Shepherd", and they called themselves "*Les Amis de la Famille Shepherd*", and it all started a long time ago, still before the war, and what they were interested in, Herr Braun said, was: *How much of the Outside World a Family must Need to Lead a Normal Civilized Life, even if stranded on an Island*. And so, without telling us anything about it, they were watching us all the time. All the time, they were recording everything about us, especially: How much of everything had been sent to us from the Outside World – how many pencils, how many aspirins, how much salt, sugar, writing paper, packing paper, lavatory paper, batteries for the radio, soap, cotton wool, needles, everything; everything, even poor Matilda, the cow, was duly documented, and she was not an ordinary cow, oh no, they had chosen a pedigree cow to be sent to us, so that they would know everything about her, who sired her, the date she was born, everything, and then, every two or three years, they sent us one of them, first it was Herr Schmied, then Herr Fischer, and now Herr Braun, to see whether we were still civilized, because, you see Mr D'Earth, they were not interested in some castaways shipwrecked on a lonely island, such as Dr Goldfinger was telling me about, no, as I've told you, what they, the Swiss, were interested in was: How-much-of-what-the-Modern-World-produces must one have to lead a decent-bourgeois-life? And so, you see, Mr D'Earth, we seem to have been very popular there, in Switzerland, *Les Amis de la Famille Shepherd* became quite fond of us, they enjoyed watching us from the distance and they were prepared to let us live on our Island indefinitely, Herr Braun said, but, alas, Herr Braun said, something had just happened that can make it *unmöglich*, Herr Braun said, by which he meant "impossible".

'And as soon as Herr Braun said that, Gregory jumped up and said, "I know what it is. It is that American, that Mr Hobson junior."

And Herr Braun said, "Yes, you guessed right, Gregory. It is because of him. He's going to force a crisis on us."

'And I said, "How's that?"

'And Herr Braun said, "He is going to lay claim to the whole Island."

'And I said, "Can he do it?"

'And he said, "Yes, he can try. He is the grandson of the original Mr Hobson, the founder."

'And Gregory said, "I'll bet he wants to make a Big Hotel out of the Big House."

'And Herr Braun said, "Well, yes, but that's not all. If that were all he wanted, you would have a chance to stay here. But . . ." – and Herr Braun turned to me, and said, "When you went to his room you saw there that French girl, Marie-Claire, sitting on his suitcase, didn't you?"

159

'And I wondered, How did he know that? And I said, "Yes, that's right. It was his suitcase she was sitting on."

'And he asked, "Do you know why she was sitting on it?"

'And I said, "No, I don't."

'And he said, "It was because when she heard your footsteps, she had no time to close the suitcase properly, so she sat on it."

'And I said, "You don't mean, Herr Braun, it was she who opened it?"

'And he said, "Of course I do. She's a clever girl. She and that boy, Pierrot. The salt of the earth. They found what they were looking for. And they have already signalled it to their bosses in France. And . . . *Lieber Gott!* Just imagine! The French government protests. A French gunboat comes to put the Tricolour on the island. The British marines rush to tear it down. An American aircraft carrier cruising in wait. The Baltic countries' submarines in *La Manche* . . ."

' "But what did they find?" I asked.

'And he said, "Well, I've told you."

'And I said, "No, you haven't, Herr Braun."

'And he said, "I haven't what?"

'And he looked so perplexed. And that was the first time that I felt him to be so very human. I mean: vulnerable. No, not vulnerable to what comes from the outside world. What I mean is: vulnerable to some spot inside himself, whatever it is. So I said gently, "You haven't told us what they found in the suitcase."

'And he said, "Actually it was the girl, Marie-Claire, who found it. And she told Pierrot, her partner. And Pierrot signalled it to France. And then Pierrot accepted a glass of schnapps which I took from *my* suitcase, and we went for a walk, and the sky was already black but the stars were bright, and the sea all around us was murmuring its dark secrets in the language known only to the sirens, and Pierrot was in a romantic mood, and he said: *How uncanny to be in a point of* space and time where one simple act you have the power to perform could prevent History from taking a road into an abyss.

' "And I asked him, *What sort of act, my Pierrot?*

' "And he said, *Bumping off.*

' "And I said, *Oh, dear . . .*

' "And he said, *Precisely.*

' "And I said, *Have you ever killed anybody, Pierrot?*

' "And he said, *No. And I wouldn't, unless they ordered me to.*

' "And so I said, *I hope they are not fools and will not.*

' "And he said he hoped they *were* fools and would not. And then he told me the whole story, he said that he and Marie-Claire are the salt of the earth, and that he knew that I was also the salt of the earth, which I neither confirmed nor denied, and that we – he said – we who are the salt of the earth, whether French or Swiss, or whatever, should be telling each other all we know, because only a knowledge of the truth can secure the peace of the earth, and the only thing that can beat the new miniature cameras, telescopic lenses, and electronic eavesdropping bugs, is to have no secrets; that because of all those modern technological devices, the new world will have to have no secrets, so I said that I quite agreed, and to show that I was willing to co-operate, I said, *You know, Pierrot, that Dr Janson is actually the deposed President of Bukumla?*

' "And he said, *Of course I know that.*

' "And I said, *But it isn't him you want to off?*

' "And he said, *No, it is not.*

' "And I said, *It can't possibly be Dr Goldfinger or Princess Zuppa, can it? Or Lady Lucy and her daughter, or the daughter's boyfriend?*

' "And he said, *I'm not quite sure about the daughter's boyfriend, but, anyway, no, it isn't him.*

And so I said, *Then it must be that young American, Mr Hobson. But why? What do you have against him? He doesn't hide that he considers himself to be the rightful owner of the Island and wants to turn the Big House into a Big Hotel. He talked to me quite openly about it.*

' "And Pierrot said, *But he didn't tell you who is behind it, did he? Ask Marie-Claire, she'll tell you. It is the American salt of the earth that backs him. It's all very cleverly planned. As soon as he gets the Island legally and has the hotel working, he sells the lot to the Yanks who'll build their naval base here. And do you think France will allow that? To have our* La Manche *corked up by them? No, Herr Braun, he said, We always think that the war will start in Libya, in the Suez Canal, in Lebanon, in Turkey, in the Gulf, in the North Pole or South Pole, and we never think that it may start on Hobson's Island."*

'It was so strange to hear all that in the middle of the night, and coming from such a sober man as Herr Braun. I didn't know what to say. But Gregory was keeping to the facts. "You told us, Herr Braun, that at the time old Mr Hobson died, the Island was no longer his property. It was a Trust. And it was for the trustees to say who was going to be the beneficiary."

' "That's right," Herr Braun said.

' "So what can he do?" Gregory asked.

' "He can litigate," Herr Braun said.

' "Meaning what?" Gregory asked.

' "Go to law. Contest the validity of the whole thing," Herr Braun said.

' "And can he do it?" Gregory asked.

' "Oh, yes," Herr Braun said.

' "After all that time?" Gregory asked.

' "Well, that's one thing against him," Herr Braun said.

' "And what's *for* him?" Gregory asked.

'To which Mr Braun said, "Well, let me tell you what he's going to do. He's going to tell the court that the whole arrangement for the Trust is invalid because his grandfather was mad at the time."

'To which Gregory asked, "Was he?"

'To which Herr Braun sighed, lifted his right hand, let it fall

162

gently on the table, and said, "How can I know? I was a little schoolboy then, dreaming of climbing Mont Blanc and writing poetry."

'So I asked him, "And did you?"

'And he said, "I didn't climb Mont Blanc."

'But Gregory said, "But can he prove it?"

'And Herr Braun said, "The old man committed suicide."

'And Gregory said, "Some very sane men commit suicide."

'And Herr Braun said, "And so do some mad men, at their *lucida intervalla*."

'And I said, "What's that?"

'And he said, "Moments of sanity."

'So I said, "Oh, dear . . ."

'And he said, "Sorry . . ."

'And Gregory said, "Now, seriously, how bad is it?"

'And Herr Braun said, "Well, you see, children, the very rules old Mr Hobson devised for the trustees might be considered mad." He looked at us, sort of sympathetically, and went on, "You see, he didn't want this Island for anybody else. He wanted it for himself, that's to say, for himself after his death. You see, children, people believe in so many fantastic things, things like playing harps in paradise or burning eternally in hell. As for him, he believed in reincarnation and metempsychosis. Millions of people in India wouldn't find anything shocking in the idea that your soul, at the death of your body, is transmigrated into a new body, human or animal, but the judges in America or Switzerland might find such ideas rather eccentric."

'So I asked him, "Do *you* believe in such things, Mr Braun?"

'And he said, "Whether I believe in them or not has nothing to do with it. I'm a lawyer. And for a lawyer, reality is what he sees black on white on paper. And what was marked black on white on paper is very difficult for the trustees to execute. Because, you see, old Mr Hobson was sure that when he died he would find his way to the Island, notwithstanding the kind

of body in which he was going to be reborn. And, consequently, if we, the trustees, do find on the Island somebody
born within twenty-four hours of Mr Hobson's death, he or
she or it must be treated as a potential beneficiary. That's why
we keep this rule so secret, because anybody who happened
to be born at the time could come to the Island and claim to
be Mr Hobson's reincarnation."

'We listened to it as if it were a fairy-tale, but it sounded
quite convincing and we just thought who could that be, and
Gregory, suddenly, exclaimed, "Nemo!"

'But Herr Braun said, "Oh, yes, we thought about him. Yet,
you see, whoever was born in 1929, the year Mr Hobson
jumped out of the window, would be only ten when the war
started and no more than fifteen when it ended. And when
Nemo appeared in his rubber dinghy during the war, he
seemed to have been a grown-up man. Unless his wartime
experiences had aged him so much. And so, to be sure, I once
asked him . . ."

'Gregory and I, we jumped. "You did what?" we exclaimed.

'And he said, "I asked him, and he told me . . ."

'Now Gregory and I, we were vying with each other
shouting, "Did you say he *told* you?! Did he actually *tell* you?!
*What* did he tell you?! We've never heard him say a word! Did
he tell you about himself? Where he comes from? Did he . . ."

'But Herr Braun said, "No, he didn't tell me where and
when he was born. The only thing he told me was that he
was happy as he was, and he didn't want to be the owner of
the Island or of anything else."

'And I asked quickly, "In what language did he tell you
that?"

'And Gregory repeated the question, "Yes, in what language
did he talk to you?"

'And we thought if we knew what his language is then we
might learn where he came from. And Herr Braun knew what
we were thinking and he smiled and said, "*Latino sine flexione*."

'Well, so that was that about Nemo. I remembered what Mr Wilkinson – that defrocked boatman who married me to Gregory – I remember what he said when he saw Nemo, he said, Oh, he himself had been a prisoner of war, in Java, and he knew a man's mind, and he would bet that when Nemo was drifting in his rubber dinghy, he had taken an oath not to say a word to anybody if he was miraculously rescued. And so, I thought, perhaps he, Nemo, thought that his oath might not apply to artificial languages, and, perhaps, who can tell? when he found in the library a book on Latin-without-inflexions he took it and learnt it? And I had mixed feelings about it, but Herr Braun said, "Please don't show him that we know about it, we are on the brink of doing something difficult and we don't need," he said, "any additional trouble."

'So I asked him, "What is that difficult thing?"

'And he said, "We must find a beneficiary, and we must do it very quickly. Before young Hobson starts the litigation. Our position will be much stronger if we can show that the Island has its legitimate owner. Because possession is nine tenths of the law."

'And I said, "But do we have one in view . . . ?"

'And he said, "Listen carefully. I have already told you that our *Societé des Amis de la Famille Shepherd* was very scrupulous about everything imported into the island. For instance, when we bought for you Matilda, the cow, she wasn't an ordinary cow, she was a pedigree cow, we knew everything about her. We knew, for instance, when she was born. Namely, that she was born the day Mr Hobson jumped out of the window."

'We gasped. We immediately saw the implication. Mr Hobson's soul transmigrating into the body of Matilda, the cow. "But poor Matilda is dead!" I said.

'To which Herr Braun said, "Yes. She's dead. But the very day she died, Nemo appeared on the island and Georgina, Gregory's sister, was born." He stopped. He observed us for a longish while and then went on, "We, the trustees, thought

165

a lot about Nemo. We thought, well, as he appeared on the Island so much out of the blue, perhaps we can consider that he was re-born on that very day. Still, that interpretation seemed to be rather forced. Besides, as I've just told you, he was not interested. And so, there remains Miss Georgina . . ."

'Now Gregory opened his mouth wide, perhaps in astonishment, but I feared he would say something unnecessary, and so I said sharply, "Shut up!"

'And Gregory was surprised because I never talked to him like that, but Herr Braun looked at me and said, "You are a wise woman, my dear."

'And Gregory still didn't seem to see what all that was about, and he looked at me as if he had never seen me before.

'And Herr Braun said, "Surely you know where she lives, surely you know how to find her."

'And I said quickly, not letting Gregory say a word, "Of course we know. Of course I can go and bring her here."

'To which Herr Braun said, "Well, then that's fine. Do so," and then he added, "I expect it is in Ireland that she lives."

'And I said, "Yes, in Ireland."

'And he said, "Well, then. My boat is still here. Take it tomorrow morning and go and fetch her." And then he said, "Before you leave you must tell your children that their aunt will be coming." And then, after a moment, he added, "It will be all right if she comes alone . . ." And so I knew that he knew and perhaps had known all those twenty years, because, as I told you, Mr D'Earth, or did I? – well, it was twenty years ago that Herr Braun came to visit us for the first time, and Gregory was so young, and our parents were dead, and Herr Braun said that he, Gregory, managed very well, and he, Herr Braun, had no complaints, but he, Gregory, is so young and sooner or later would want to leave the Island to see the world and to marry, to which, on the spur of the moment, he, Gregory, said that he had a fiancée who was willing to live on the Island, and so, when Herr Braun left, we discussed the problem and I went to Dublin, and then to Belfast, and then to Liverpool, and then to London where I changed my hairstyle and came back to the Island as Miss Geraldine Stubbs and made a defrocked boatman from the Scilly Islands marry me to my brother Gregory with whom I have lived now for twenty years and had three children and am pregnant with one more, and so now I decided to go away again and come back as Georgina, Gregory's sister, and my children's aunt, and Herr Braun said I was a wise woman, and then he said it was late and we all needed some sleep before the busy day started, and I saw him to the door, and the sky was very black still, but the stars were very bright, and as Herr Braun was walking towards the Big House, and the sea was calm, the southern breeze brought to my ears the strange sound of something like some torn-out-bits of giggling, and I realized that I had again forgotten to tell Herr Braun about the Menace of the Ship, and I wanted to run just those few steps after him and tell him, but I didn't, and that's how history is unpredictable, that's to say, because historians cannot know whether somebody on a lonely island will run a few steps or will not.'

## EIGHT

## 'Tee-hee-hee Ha ha ha Hoo hoo hoo'

'I'm frightened, Mr D'Earth. Please hold my hand please, I'm so frightened.'

She stretched her left hand towards him, and he pulled his armchair an inch nearer the bed and took her clenched fist in his two hands, and that clenched fist was a strange object, so white, cold, and anatomically complicated, he looked at it and could hardly recognize what it was. Once upon a time, when he was a young boy in that village on the border of Sussex and Surrey, he had held a frog in his hands, and the frog was green, cold, and so strange because there was *a* life in it; and then the frog jumped and there was nothing. And now, the hand he held between his hands was also strange, it was also cold, but there was no life in it, it was asking for life, and so he kept it enveloped in his palms, but he didn't like it, it was such a strange object, that hand, white, cold, and so complicated, anatomically. Why do people hold hands, he mused, why do they feel it reassuring? Is it psychological, purely? Or does something physical, some heat exchange, or what not, take place somewhere there? He looked at his own hands. The skin was wrinkled, there were a few hairs on it, and some brown spots.

'Tell me,' he said, 'what was he like?'

'Who?' she asked.

'That young American. Hobson,' he said.

'Oh,' she said. 'Young. Good-looking. Businesslike.'

'Did he say anything about his father?'

'About his grandfather?'

'No, not grandfather. Father.'

'No, he didn't.'

'And about his mother?'

'No,' she said.

'You don't know whether she's still alive?'

'No,' she said.

Well, it doesn't matter, does it? Poor Prickly Rose. Alive? Dead? What does it matter? What does it matter, indeed! Nemesis or coincidence? Hadn't his son, Adam, asked him the other day, Had his mother had any more children, any Hobson children? Well, he, Sean D'Earth, had never divorced Prickly Rose, therefore her Hobson son would be a bastard, which doesn't mean that he can't inherit from his grandfather, does it? And so what? Vulgar trivia. Trivial vulgarity. Vulvia trigar. Garvial tri . . . he half-closed his eyes, but opened them again quickly when she withdrew her hand and laughed. This time he had no doubts. It *was* laughter. A very short burst of . . . yes, definitely, of laughter. He was puzzled. It was so incongruous. He repeated to himself the word 'incongruous'. How stange, he wondered, do minds hold hands as bodies do? Because the word 'incongruous' was not an everyday word, and yet, as soon as it appeared in his mind, she used it:

'Do you think, Mr D'Earth, that if something *incongruous* happens to a pregnant woman, it will pass down to the child?'

'What sort of thing?' he asked.

She didn't answer.

Suddenly, he wanted to go back. It was he, Sean D'Earth, who, suddenly, wanted to go back. Decades and decades back. Back to the little village on the Sussex and Surrey border, back to the deliciously melancholy sadness of his childhood, – indeed, what was he doing here, sitting in this strange (his own) armchair, in this strange (his own) room, in this strange (his own) house, with this strange woman in front of him, lying on his bed, and giggling. Because she had giggled,

169

hadn't she? And yet, when he held it in his hands, wasn't her hand cold with fear?

'So you left the Island as Mrs Shepherd and went back as Miss Shepherd . . .' he said.

'No, no. Not yet,' she said. 'I had to talk to my children first. I had to assure them that everything would be as it was, everything would be fine, no difference at all, but when I come back they mustn't call me Mummy. They must call me *Aunt*. Or Georgina. Or Gina. Anything except "Mother". They were very excited about it. "Oh, Mummy," they said, "how very funny!"

'And then Philip said, "Can you bring me something, Mum?"

'And I said, "I'm afraid, Philip, this time I might be in a hurry. May have no time."

'But he insisted, "But if you can find time, it's important."

'So I asked him, "What is it?"

'And he said, "A computer."

'And it was so unexpected that I nearly laughed. And I thought of those people in Switzerland, those *Amis de la Famille Shepherd*, who would have to add the item "computers" to their list of things a family must receive from the outside world to be able to lead a normal, civilized life.

'But then Philip repeated, "I need a computer, *Mum!*"

'And there was something in the way he said it that I didn't like. Especially, the way he said the word "Mum".

And Jane noticed it too. It sounded as if he was blackmailing me, as if he meant to say, "If you don't bring me a computer, I'm going to call you *Mum*." And Jane gripped his ear and said, "You must swear that you'll call her *Aunt!*" And he said "Let go! Take your hands off me," but she didn't, she said, "Repeat after me: *I cross my heart and may I die, if I so much as tell a lie*." And he said, "I cross my heart and may I die, if I so much as tell a lie," and then he laughed and said, "And it would be a lie if I called her *Aunt*," and Jane said, "No it wouldn't, she is our father's sister, so she is our aunt, isn't she?" And Louise said, "Philip, if you don't behave, I'll take the breakfast tray to Dr Janson tomorrow morning." and Philip said, "You bitch," and started to cry.

'And so, you see, dear Mr D'Earth, it wasn't so easy, after all. Anyway. I packed my suitcase, I found some of my twenty-year-old things and was pleased they still fitted me, but it was with a heavy heart that I embarked . . .'

She shut her eyes and said, 'Well, if I must, I must. If I must tell you, then I must tell you. But it isn't easy. When one delays putting into words things that have happened, it is a bit as if one were delaying the very fact of their having happened, and if the fact is delayed, then there is something like a hope that they may still not happen, while putting things in words is like nailing the coffin, and . . .' Tears began to flow from her eyes, but she was *not* crying. Her breathing was normal and the tone of her voice was evenly quiet, as before. 'Don't worry, dear Mr D'Earth,' she went on, 'I'll tell you everything I know. I need to tell it *out*, out of myself, if you see what I mean, Mr D'Earth, and I'll be quick now, Mr D'Earth, you see, the boat, you know, the boat that brought Herr Braun was still there, and Herr Braun told the old skipper to take me, Mr Gregory's wife, to Ireland and bring back Mr Gregory's sister. And so we went and I stopped for the night in a hotel and registered there as Mrs Gregory Shepherd, and the next day I went to a beauty parlour and changed my hair-style and put on some bright vulgar make-up, and spent the next night in another hotel where I registered as Miss Georgina Shepherd, and early in the morning went back to the harbour, to my boat, and the skipper said, "You Mr Gregory's sister?" and I said, "Aye," and he said, "You look much like his wife, do you know that?" and I said, "It was because she looked like me that my brother married her." And he accepted that and said to his son who was his only crew, "Cook us some breakfast, Sonny," and the son said, "Aye aye, Skipper," and that was that.

'Dear, dear Mr D'Earth. Can you imagine that all that was only yesterday? I can't. I can't believe it was yesterday morning and not a hundred years ago. The sea was still, the sun was shining, I stood on the deck heading now already due south, and the moment I saw the northern tip of the island on the horizon, I thought: this is going to be mine, the whole of it is going to be mine, I'm going to be an isle owner, I'm going to be the Dame of Hobson's Island! Oh, dear, dear Mr D'Earth. We all think we are above such things, and we are, we really are, but only so long as we have no chance. Because let a Herr Braun whisper something in our ear and we discover such unexpected things about ourselves. Well, my elation didn't last long. "Look, Dad!" the skipper's son shouted. We turned our heads, and there, from the east, a boat was coming at great speed towards us. We just couldn't make out what she was. A lifeboat? No. A fireservice launch? No. A police patrol? No. The customs? The Royal Navy? Pirates? They signalled us to stop, and we slowed down. In no time at all they were quite close to our starboard. Three men on the deck. "Where are you headed for?" they shouted.

' "Hobson's Island," we said.

' "No, you are not," they said. "Turn round and go back where you come from!"

' "What's all this about?" we said.

' "Wise people don't ask questions," they said. "Off you go! We are in command here. On your bike!"

'And so I screamed, "Not so fast, mister! This is my island! My name is Shepherd. I live there." I winked to our skipper. "I'm going home and you can't stop me!"

'So the three men on the deck conferred with each other for a minute, and then said "OK. You come with us, madam, and the rest go home."

'The boats were now alongside, the gap between them

narrowed, and when they came close enough to bump gunwales, I jumped on to their deck. Then the skipper's son handed me my suitcase, and that was that.

'A minute later, as we headed for the Island, I told them, "You'll find a jetty in the middle of the eastern seafront."

' "Is that so?" they said, as if they had their doubts about the very thought that such a thing as a jetty could exist on what was marked as "danger rocks" on the Admiralty charts.

'Two of the three men were sailors, naturally. The third one didn't look like a sailor. I shall not describe him to you, dear Mr D'Earth, because you know him well. It was your son. They called him Sir Adam,' she said, and paused.

'Please go on,' Sean D'Earth said.

She hesitated. Then she took a deep breath and said, 'I didn't know, of course, who he was. He looked at me carefully, as if I were a specimen of something or other, and then we left the other two men standing on the deck, and he took me below. In the cabin, he said, "You are Mrs Shepherd."

'I myself didn't know any more, was I Mrs or Miss Shepherd, but I said, "That's right."

'So he said, "And you say you live on the Island."

'So I said again, "That's right."

'And he said "You don't live alone on the Island, or do you?"

'I said, "No, of course not."

'So he said, "Who else lives there?"

'I was all mixed up. Didn't know whether I should call Greg my brother or my husband, so I said, "Gregory and the children. Louise who is eighteen, Jane who is seventeen, and Philip – fifteen."

'And he said, "Jesus!"

'And I said, "And there is Nemo."

'And he asked, "Who is Nemo?"

'So I said, "Our old gardener."

'So he said, "Jesus!" and then he said, "That's all?"

'So I said, "Yes. Except for the visitors."

'So he said, "Are you having some visitors just now?"

'So I said, "Yes, lots of them."

'So he said, "Jesus!" And then he said, "Who are they?"

'So I said, "There's Dr Janson, the deposed President of Bukumla."

'So he said, "Jesus!"

'And I said, "And there is Herr Braun. He is Swiss. A trustee of the Island."

'And he said again, "Jesus!"

'And I said, "And there is an Italian lady called Princess Zuppa, and her friend Dr Goldfinger, and a couple of French secret agents, called Marie-Claire and Pierrot."

'And he said, "Jesus!"

'And I said, "And there's an American, called Hobson, he says he's the grandson of the founder."

'And he said, "Bloody hell!"

'And not knowing of course that Lady Lucy is his wife and Deborah his daughter, I said, "And there is a British secret service woman called Lady Lucy, and her daughter who is a poet, and the daughter's friend, called John."

'And now I knew there was something that was very wrong because he didn't say "Jesus" and he didn't say "Bloody hell" but his face turned as white as a sheet. And then he asked, "When were you there last? When did you leave the Island?"

'And that was again a difficult question for me to answer. Because, if I was Miss Shepherd then I left the Island twenty years ago. But if I was Mrs Shepherd then I left the Island two days ago. I thought for a second and decided I was Mrs Shepherd, and I said, "Two days ago."

'And he asked, "And things were normal then, nothing unusual?"

'And I said, "No, except for so many visitors, which was unusual."

174

'And he said, "Nothing else? You hadn't seen any monkeys, for instance?"

'And I asked, "Any what?!"

'And he said, "Monkeys."

'And I don't know what I thought, and I said, "No, no monkeys. We don't have any monkeys on the Island."

'And he said, "Good," and he sighed. And relaxed a little. And I, I don't know why, I thought of the maternity hospital in Ireland, and then, again I don't know what made me, but I said, "You know, Sir Adam, (they called him Sir Adam, so I too called him Sir Adam), you know, Sir Adam," I said, "I've never seen a monkey. I know, of course, what they look like, but I don't know what they sound like. If at all."

'And he asked, "Why do you say that?"

'And I said, "I don't know. I heard some noises during the night, when the sea was calm."

'And he asked, "What kind of noises?"

'And I said, "Tee-hee-hee Ha ha ha Hoo hoo hoo."

'And he asked, "Where were they coming from?"

'And I said, "From a ship, anchored off the southern tip of the Island."

'And he said, "Jesus! Let's hope they are still there."

'And at that moment the boat touched the jetty, and he said, "You can leave your suitcase here, you won't need it for the moment," and he went up, and he told the captain to go and stay at some distance from the shore and not come back till he was given a signal, and he took from his pocket something that looked like a pistol and wasn't, and he aimed it vertically up to the sky, and a thin straight fibre of light appeared above it for no longer than half a second, and then we jumped on to the jetty, and the boat started moving away, and I said, "It's funny that nobody is here to greet us."

'and he said, "Should they be?"

'and I said, "We usually do when we see a boat coming."

'and then he said something strange, he said, "Keep your gloves on" (Yes, I was wearing my gloves),

'and I said, "All right",

'and he said something stranger still, he said, "If you see a monkey, don't let him touch you, and don't touch him."

'And now I thought he was mad. And I asked him, "And what will happen if I do?"

'And he said, "You'll die of laughter."

## NINE

## And the Virgin said, 'Ha!'

'As I said, Mr D'Earth, I thought that your son was mad. In a way I was right. And, in a way, I was wrong. As I see it now, yes, he must have been mad for a long time before all that. But then and there, as he put his feet on the Island, he was quite sane. Sane? Did I say "sane"? Is there anything in this mad world one may call sane? No. No. I'm so confused. Perhaps I shouldn't have said that he became sane. Perhaps I should have said that his madness had gone. Or, perhaps I shouldn't have said even that. Perhaps what I should have said was that his madness had lost its battle.

'The truth is that I was frightened. I had never been frightened before. Not on the Island. Not in that sort of way. When I was a little girl, I would go out in the middle of the night to stand on the very edge of the shore and look at the big waves coming towards me from the darkness of the end of the world, I would be knocked senseless by a feeling for which I wouldn't have a name, but it was never a feeling of fright. And now I *was* frightened. Just because nobody had come to greet us . . .

'I told you, Mr D'Earth – didn't I? – that I was part of the Island. It wasn't just a way of saying it. I *was* her part, I had her feelings, I had her thoughts. And what did I do? First, I left her, as Gregory's wife, and then I came back, as Gregory's sister, to claim to be my island's *Owner*, to claim to be her *Dame*. No wonder she was rejecting me now, no wonder she was greeting me now with what felt like a big, overwhelming Absence. And fear.

'And so we stood on the jetty for a couple of minutes, and

then your son said, "Where do we go from here?" and I said, "We go to the farmhouse," and I took him to the farmhouse, and there was nobody there, we walked from room to room and there was nobody, no Gregory, no Louise, no Jane, no Philip, and as I still wasn't sure who was I, there was no Geraldine if I was Georgina, and there was no Georgina if I was Geraldine.

'Now, whatever has happened, let's face it, I told myself, and "Come," I said to your son and I led him across the garden to the shed. We called it "the shed" because once upon a time Matilda, the cow, used to live there, till the day she died, the very day I was born and Nemo appeared on the Island and made his home there, in the shed. He had rebuilt it since, completely, but we went on calling it "the shed", nevertheless. And so I went with your son to the shed, and we looked in. There was nobody there. The red carpet was hanging on the wall, as before, but I noticed that mother's photograph – which, as I told you, he had pinned in the middle of it – was missing. And so your son said, "It seems there's nobody here," and there was a note of hope in his voice, as if he thought – perhaps what I had told him was a fairy-scary story and the Island was really a desert island as she was meant to be.

'Now, if you look at the Island from the jetty, which is on the east coast, the Big House is on your left, and the farmhouse – a bit further up and on your right, and so it was, only now, as we were coming back, approaching the Big House from the west, that I noticed a big poster hanging on its west wall. I knew at once that it could have been done by nobody but Deborah and her friend John. It read in big letters:

POETRY READING
by
Archangel Gabriel
&

178

*And the Virgin said, 'Ha!'*

the Virgin
in person

'They are all in the Big House,' I said. 'Let's go,' I said, and
we moved to the main entrance that leads, you know, to that
big Hall of such a curious shape that nobody knew, you know,
what its destination was ever meant to be.

'And when we stopped by the door, I heard plenty of
laughter, and I relaxed, thinking they must be reciting some
funny poems, perhaps a bit naughty, they wouldn't laugh at
such lines as –

> *Her* lips were red, *her* looks were free,
> Her locks were yellow as gold:
> Her skin was white as leprosy,
> The Night-mare LIFE-IN-DEATH was she,
> Who thicks man's blood with cold,

– would they? But your son's face was grim, and he took
out of his pocket that gadget that looked like a pistol but
wasn't, and I said, "What do you need that for?" but he didn't
answer and pushed the door open.

They were all over the place, sitting, standing, lying on the
floor, and laughing on and on. And on and on. And on and
on. And on and on. And, at first, it seemed funny, and I
wanted to join them in laughing, and I wanted to know what
it was that made them laugh so con-su-med-ly, and I looked
at your grand-daughter Deborah and her friend John, they
were standing on some packing cases, she, the Virgin, stood
there very stiff, unsmiling, but saying "Ha!" every fifth
second, 1,2,3,4,Ha! 1,2,3,4,Ha!, and I still thought it was a sort
of poetry, and he, John Ostel, the Archangel Gabriel, had big
wings made of silver paper, and he looked as if his mouth
were filled with laughter, but what he was saying wasn't
funny at all, no, not at all, it made me feel as if something had
happened to my throat, you know, a spasm, you know . . . O

179

yes, Mr D'Earth, don't worry, yes, I'll tell you what he said, John, the Archangel Gabriel. O yes . . .

'He spread his silver-paper wings and said, "He? He was not a water-lily floating on the surface of the pond . . ."

'And your grand-daughter, Deborah the Virgin, said, "Ha!"

'And he said, "Neither was He a daddy-long-legs, nor a pondskater, not a waterstrider supported by surface tension of water . . ."

'And the Virgin said, "Ha!"

' "His weight was 10 stone and the area of the sole of His foot was 20 square inches," he went on . . .

'And the Virgin said, "Ha!"

' "Which makes half-a-stone per square inch . . ."

'And the Virgin said, "Ha!"

' "And yet He walked on water. And His walking on water was not a parable. His walking on water was a physical fact."

'And the Virgin said, "Ha!"

' "And the story of Lazarus whom He brought back to life without the help of the National Health Lazarettos, was not a parable. It was a physical fact."

'And the Virgin said, "Ha!"

' "And His chucking the monetarists out of the synagogue was not a parable. It was a physical fact."

'And the Virgin said, "Ha!"

' "And His whole life was not a parable, it was a physical fact."

'And the Virgin said, "Ha!"

' "It is your bloody lives that are a parable, not His!" he yelled, and his mouth was still filled with laughter, and his tongue with bitterness.

'And the Virgin said, "Ha!"

'And it was frightening.

'You know . . .

'It was very frightening.

'And then, from high above, from a little gallery under the

180

lofty ceiling, came a high-pitched voice: "Tee-hee-hee Ha ha ha Hoo hoo hoo."

'We looked up and saw a little monkey hanging by its tail from the balustrade of the gallery and screaming, "Tee hee hee Ha ha ha Hoo hoo hoo," and your son lifted that gadget of his that looked like a pistol but wasn't, and he directed it at the monkey, and a bright yellow streak of light appeared for a fraction of a second between it and the little monkey, and the little monkey fell down on the floor, and none of them stopped laughing, Herr Braun and Princess Zuppa and Dr Goldfinger and Dr Janson and the American and Lady Lucy and Pierrot and Marie-Claire and Gregory and Louise and Jane, they all went on laughing in their different ways, and then I saw Philip, my son Philip, and he was lying on the floor, and I knew that he was dead, he was dead, my son Philip, and his dead body was laughing, and its laughter was fraught with pain, and his body was lying by the side of the body of the little monkey, and all those things happening one on top of another and so fast got confused in my poor mind, and I shouted to your son, "You've killed him! You've killed my son Philip!" and I wanted to run to him, to my son, to my little son, but your big son held me fast, "You can't do that," he said. "You mustn't touch anything here. Unless you want your unborn baby to die of laughter in your womb." That was what he said, and he seized me from behind, pinning my elbows, and marched me out of the building.

'It was not far from there to the jetty, but there were some trees in front of the Big House, and monkeys – I don't know how many – were sitting in their branches, and we had to run because they were throwing something at us, I don't know what, maybe their own monkey dung, and as we were running, your son was aiming at them his gadget that looked like a pistol and wasn't, and I didn't look back and didn't know if he had killed any, and then – no more trees, no more trees near the jetty, no more trees for monkeys to sit on, so we stood there, on the jetty, panting, and the men on the deck of the boat far away must have seen the streaks of yellow light and thought it was a signal for them to come, and the boat started moving towards us, but she was still far away, and your son said to me, "Now you must do exactly as I tell you," and I was completely drained of my own will, and I said, "Yes," and he said, "You'll go now on board the boat, they will take you to Penzance, they will put you on the night train to London, and, once there, you'll go straight from the station to see my father." And he gave me your address. "It is not far from Paddington Station," he said, and my mind was completely empty of my own thoughts, and of my own feelings, and I said, "Yes," and then he said, "You'll go and see my father, and you will tell him four things. You'll tell him *one* that I love him and have always loved him, *two* that he was right, *three* that I was wrong, *four* that I am sorry. Now repeat what you have to say. One?"

'And so I said, "That you love him and have always loved him."

'And he said, "Two?"

'And I said, "That he was right." (I mean you.)

'And he said, "Three?"

'And I said, "That you were wrong." (I mean he.)

'And he said, "Four?"

'And I said, "That you are sorry." (I mean he).

'And then he told me that I must not only not tell anybody what I saw, but I must not let them even think that I saw or knew anything, because all those things were the most secret scientific War Department secrets, so if they suspected that I knew something or if they knew that I suspected something, they'd find a way of silencing me, that's what he said, "silencing you" (I mean me), and so if the men on the boat asked me what I was doing on the Island, I must say something like – I went to a poetry-reading, and that's all. And I said, "All right, but . . ." And I said *but* because there was something I couldn't understand. So I said, "But why did those other two men let the mad monkeys loose on our island, if they knew that it was inhabited?"

'He looked at me and asked, "How do you know they knew?"

'So I said, "Of course they knew. Their ship was anchored off the southern tip, but they came ashore, two or them, spent a night in a tent they pitched there, and as they were rather rude, we chucked them out, and 'It will be your funeral' one of them said when they were leaving."

'And, as he heard that, your son said, "Jesus!" and he looked as if it was news to him. And I thought, could it have been that they had revenged themselves on us? Could it have been that they had revenged themselves on us because they felt humiliated? Could it have been that they had revenged themselves on us because they were humilated by Dr Janson, who did the chucking out, could it have been because they were humiliated by a black man?

'I didn't mention any of it because at that moment the boat touched our jetty, your son started talking to the skipper, giving him instructions, I was at once whisked aboard, after which your son said to me, "Bless you," and then he turned round and, brandishing that gadget that looked like a pistol but wasn't, he walked away and we shoved off.

'There were only two of them, the skipper and the crew, and it was the crew that looked like the boss. They did ask me about the Island, what I was doing there. "We went to see a silly poetry recital," I said, keeping my face straight, and they didn't ask any more questions and wanted me to go below, to the cabin, and have a rest, but I refused. I stood on the deck and didn't feel at all that we were moving; it was my Island that moved, sailed further and further away and little by little was becoming smaller and smaller till the sense of my life was swallowed by the horizon. And then I turned my head the other way and saw the dinghy.

'Oh yes, it was *the* dingy. The same, some forty-year-old yellowish reddish rubber dinghy. And the man in it must have been Nemo. Nemo! So that's why I hadn't seen him in the Big House. Nemo! I hadn't even noticed his absence, and now he was there, in his old rubber dinghy, and all my love, my life, my hope, went to him, Nemo! "There's a man in a dinghy!" I shouted. "Quick! It's an old rubber dinghy. We must rescue him!"

'They came to my side of the boat and they looked, and the skipper said, "There's no dinghy in view, madam." And I knew he was lying, and I said, "But look there, have you no humanity left in you?" And he said to the crew, "Bring me my spy-glass." And the crew, who was the boss, brought him the binoculars, and he looked through them, and said, "There are no bloody dinghies there, look yourself, madam," and he pressed the binoculars to my eyes so that I couldn't see anything, and the crew who was the boss put something wet and smelly under my nose, and that was all I remembered when I woke to find myself lying in the cabin, the two men helping me to get up, saying, "We've arrived, madam, you must hurry up, not to miss the night train."

'And I said, "Is he here?"

'And they asked, "Who, madam?"

'And I said, "The man in the dinghy."

'And they said, "There was no man in a dinghy, madam. You must have seen it in your dream, madam."

'And I knew they were lying, but I couldn't do anything. They took me to the railway station, the first-class sleeping car, and, as the train started, I told myself, All right, I'll do as your son asked, I'll go and see you, and the first thing I'll tell you will be that I want to die. And it was such a great and quieting thought, the thought that I'd go and see you and say that I want to die, and I came to see you, Mr D'Earth, and as you closed the door behind me and said, "Do come in," I put my suitcase down and said, "I want to die," and you said,

"We all do," and I asked, "So why don't we?" and you said, "Because of the body. The mystery of the body. Or the chemistry of the body. Or both." '

She stopped.

And then she said, 'That's the whole story, Mr D'Earth,' and, as he didn't answer, she looked sideways at him, as he was sitting there in his armchair so near the bed on which she was lying in his bathrobe, and said 'But you are not listening . . .'

'O yes, I am,' he said. 'And I not only hear what you say, I *see* it.'

'But your eyes are closed,' she said.

'I hear with my hearing-aid open and see with my eyes closed,' he said.

## TEN

## Four Laws of Levitation and the Barbecue Machine

He heard with his hearing-aid open, and he saw with his eyes closed. What he heard was – again and again – what Mrs Shepherd had just told him, on and on, sounding, resounding, re-echoing, refusing to go away; and what he saw was the Big House's Poetry Reading Hall filled with laughter, the laughter of death. And he was there where was what he saw.

Then the telephone rang once more, but what he heard was the sound of gunshots. Not pistol shots – cracking. Big calibre guns – booming. He rushed out of where he saw that he was, turned to the right, and stopped. There was the way under the trees which Mrs Shepherd had been describing, the way she and his son Adam took only yesterday (Only yesterday!) the way to go from the Big House to the jetty. But now it was the Way of the Little Monkeys, little dead monkeys, so many dead little monkeys stigmatized with a *sardonicus risus, risus mortis*, so many dead little monkeys all along the road to the jetty. He walked gingerly, so as not to touch them.

The telephone went on ringing, but what he heard was the big guns again. And, as he now stood on the jetty, facing the sea, he saw it all: On his right – a French gunboat, proudly displaying her *drapeau tricolore*, the smoke still hanging at *la bouche* of her *canons de marine*. And in front of her, just in front of his eyes, *The Resurrection*, with bleeding holes in her body, sinking.

What is she doing here?

Why has she come back?

Has her master, Captain Pain-in-the-neck, gone mad?

Has he converted her into a pleasure boat, full of sightseers who are now, panic-stricken, jumping into the sea to swim ashore to Hobson's Island?

Jumping into the sea to swim ashore to Hobson's Island.

He is horrified.

He wants to warn them.

The swimmers.

He wants to tell them the horrid truth that . . . Once they step on Hobson's Island they will be bound to die, and to die of laughter.

They will be bound to die, and to die of laughter.

But the truth is stuck in his contracted throat, because he knows, he knows that for them there is no alternative.

For them, it is: To die of laughter on Hobson's Island or to sink with *The Resurrection*.

To die of laughter or to sink.

•

And now the echo of John's preaching resounds in his hearing-aid. Poor John . . . He remembers him. He remembers poor John, a little schoolboy who despised and hated his own father, that Great Man of Letters . . . Oh, yes, he remembers John, poor John, whose sister had trained a black poodle to carry bombs and then escaped to a guru in India; John who was to write a thesis on Samuel Beckett and ended by having a nervous breakdown; John who was arrested when trying to have a pee in front of a closed warehouse in one of the little streets off Edgware Road and, enraged, decided to improve the mores of the police by joining the Force (if you can't beat them, join them); poor John who couldn't endure it for more than a year and left and got a job of buying and selling houses; John who drifted off into the young people's pub-theatricals where he met Deborah with whom he went rowing a boat on the Serpentine; that nice, gentle John Ostel who didn't know

anything about Adam and Adam's Ha! Ha! Military Secret
Service Monkey Business, and ended by believing that all
those macabre happenings in the Big House were the result
of his own performance, and went mad, and is now preaching
to those dying of laughter:

'You think the Virgin was a parable – no! The Virgin is real,
it is you who are a parable!

'You think that I am John Ostel pretending to be the Archangel Gabriel – no, you're wrong! I *am* the Archangel Gabriel
who pretended to be John Ostel, and it is I, now, who do
slaine and slahter your sad souls with my sweord of hleahtor!'
The sword of laughter.

•

He switches off his hearing-aid and the echo of the Big House's
Poetry Reading mercifully recedes. But his closed eyes still see
the sea full of swimming sinners –
did he say 'sinners'?
And who is he to call people sinners?
Men and women.
So many women.
And girls.
And boys.
In the sea.
Swimming.
Between Hobson's Island and *The Resurrection*.
Between *The Resurrection* and the Island.
Oh, no, please!
Let it not be true!
He must be dreaming.
Of course he is dreaming.
His eyes are closed, are they not?
And if it is a dream then it can be stopped.
It will be enough to wake up to stop it, will it not?

188

## Four Laws of Levitation

And so he now dreams that he is waking up, he's sitting in his armchair, in his room, in front of the bed, and he dreams that he sits in his armchair in his room in front of the bed and says, 'I'm sorry, Mrs Shepherd, I've just had a little nap,' and as she doesn't answer, he dreams that he opens his eyes to look at her, and she is not there, not lying on his bed, and he calls, 'Mrs Shepherd! Where are you, dear?!' and as she doesn't answer, he gets up and goes to another room, and another, and another, and another, and another, and to the bathroom, and to the kitchen, actually he is visiting more rooms than there are in his house, but Mrs Shepherd isn't there, isn't anywhere, and it occurs to him in his dream that if he were dreaming (which he dreams that he is not) then the old *lapsus linguae* Insinuator for burning psychological rubbish would incinerate that his crafty walking through a suite of rooms means a wishfulthinking brothel or a harem or (according to the rule of opposites) marriage, which, of course, has nothing to do with the disappearance of Mrs Shepherd, and this reminds him of her suitcase, he himself put it by the bed, and so he goes back to the room where the bed is, but the suitcase is not there, she must have taken it with her, which is quite natural, but – with it or without it – how could she walk out of here? He goes to the hall, looks at the door, she couldn't possibly have walked through the front door. When she came in, she entered through it, didn't she? Consequently, for her, it is the entrance door.

And entrance is not exit.

Entrance and exit are contraries.

Therefore Entrance-door is not Exit-door.

And she couldn't possibly have left through it.

That's logical.

And thus, if logically she couldn't walk out, then logically she must be still in.

But empirically he cannot find her anywhere.

Therefore she must have left empirically.

But how did she manage to leave empirically so that it wouldn't contradict the logic of the door?

He wonders.

And then he goes from the hall to the room.

And he looks at the window.

The window is closed.

Oh dear, he says to himself, it's so obvious, one always forgets the most obvious things. The obvious thing is that she levitated.

She levitated.

And when one levitates one can pass through a windowpane without breaking it, just like light can pass through a windowpane without breaking it, even such light that carries with itself a picture of a big elephant or a thick-skinned rhinoceros with two horns on its snout, we all know well that it will pass through without breaking the windowpane, that's the *First Law of Nature (re: Levitation)*, it is a very well-known law of nature, it says that when you levitate you can pass through glass like light does, and, surely, that was how Mrs Shepherd went out of here, and he will do the same, it's so obvious and so easy, first you levitate – he is already one inch above the floor, you see?, ten inches, it's so simple! he's already under the ceiling, he changes his position to horizontal, makes a gentle breaststroke, and he is already outside, moving higher in the lovely fresh air, under the blue sky, because this is the *Second Law of Nature (re: Levitation)*, it says that when you levitate the sky is always blue and the sun is always shining, and no sound disturbs you, aeroplanes go to Heathrow and from Heathrow silently, helicopters hover around you and above you and below you silently, and no radar can detect you, you are free, you are free to float to . . . and see for yourself . . .

To float where to?

To see what?

Oh yes, he knows, he knows very well, he couldn't name

it at the moment, but he doesn't need to name it, he knows without naming it, when one levitates one doesn't need a rudder to go where one wants to go, and a very little power takes you miles and miles, and he has plenty of power, mental power and will power, enough to go there and come back, he is already half-way there, and the blue sky is very blue and the bright sun is very bright and the lulled sea has rocked itself to slumber and now, all of a sudden, a big white seagull with a big yellow beak – coming straight towards him, Oh no!, it's too late, he can't outmanoeuvre the seagull, its beak is already in his breast, the whole bird has already passed through him and is sailing away, and he knows that this is the *Third Law of Nature (re: Levitation)*, namely: that when you levitate, things will pass through you like light passes through glass, and they and you will be the same as before. And so he is as he was before, and the seagull is as it was before, and the seagull continues in its direction, and he continues in his direction, and he knows what his direction is, he knows where what-he-goes-to is, it is 100 miles from Cornwall, and 100 miles from Ireland, and 200 miles from France, and he remembers its name now, its name is Hobson's Island, and he knows why he is going there, Oh yes, he does, though he can't put it into words, and, anyway, it is already down there, and Mrs Shepherd was right, it isn't the Admiralty chart's 'dangerous rocks', it is a pretty island, there, 800 feet below, 600 feet, from so-far-up it looks peaceful, *'As idle as a painted* island *Upon a painted sea'*, Mrs Shepherd had a good ear for words, must have found out that what Captain Pain-in-the-neck quoted was Coleridge, because she also quoted those other lines, terrifying lines, the lines that thick 'man's blood with cold', didn't she? But there is nothing terrifying now, the sky is blue and the sun is shining as he goes down, just a little, to see better, and a little more, good, he's now some 400 feet above the Island,

hovers over it,

191

very good,

oh yes,

this is the jetty she talked about, and that, there, must be
the Big House, so many aerials on the roof!, and there, further
up, west by north, the farmhouse, and the orchard, and the
shed, and the beehives . . . wait a moment . . . what is that
clearing surrounded by the trees? Mrs Shepherd has never
mentioned a clearing, and there it is, a clear glade, and a big
table in the centre, and people, people sitting round the table,
'My goodness!', it's Adam's wife, Lucy, sitting there, and
Deborah! (his adorable Deborah!) and John sitting beside her,
yes, he recognizes the three, Lucy, Deborah and John, because
he knows them, but who are the others? – he has to guess,
and he can guess it easily: that well-groomed oldish
gentleman, surely, he is Herr Braun, the Swiss banker-lawyer
(did Mrs Shepherd say something about his wife? It would be
easy to levitate to Switzerland and learn more about the Braun
family and the *Societé des Amis de la Famille Shepherd*), and,
sitting next to Herr Braun, Princess Zuppa and, surely, Dr
Goldfinger (curious name: *Zuppa*, is it short for *Zuppardi*? And
why *Princess*? Was she married to a prince? Or was her mother
a Principessa?), and next to them Gregory and his children,
unmistakably, Jane (a buxom girl) and Philip and Louise, and
next to her Dr Janson, the ex-President of Bukumla (Bukumla?
Bukumla? Why does the name *Bukumla* make him think of
Lady Cooper? And the bookshop in Praed Street? Anyway, it
doesn't matter. The chap is quite black and his mouth is full
of gold teeth and who would have guessed he was a half-
brother of Princess Zuppa?), and then, the young couple next
to him must be Pierrot and Marie-Claire, and the young man
between her and Lucy – oh dear! – mustn't he be the American
Mr Hobson junior, old Prickly Rose's son, Adam's half-
brother!

He hovers over the table and starts counting:

Lucy,

Deborah,
John,
Herr Braun,
Princess Zuppa,
Dr Goldfinger,
Gregory,
Jane,
Philip,
Louise,
Dr Janson,
Pierrot,
Marie-Claire,
Mr Hobson,
Lucy . . .

Fifteen. No, he has already counted Lucy. So it is fourteen. He doesn't like the number. Not a *prime*. It's one too many or else somebody is missing.

Who is missing?

Nemo, of course. He has never seen Nemo, but none of those around the table can be Nemo, he's sure of that. Nemo and his rubber dinghy must have drowned in the wake of the boat that was taking Mrs Shepherd to Cornwall. And so Nemo is missing.

And Mrs Shepherd is missing. She must have gone to some maternity hospital. That's why she's not here. Obviously. And then, well, what about Adam? Adam isn't here either.

He is glad that his son, Adam, is not here. His son, Adam, sent him a message saying that he loved him. Mrs Shepherd brought it. And if his son, Adam, was here, now, he, Sean D'Earth, his father, would be tempted to tell him that he doesn't care a damn whether his son loves him or not, which would be embarrassing to both, and, thus, he's glad that his son, Adam, isn't here; but if he isn't here, where is he?

He looks down at the fourteen people sitting round the table . . . What are they waiting for? Why aren't they talking?

Why aren't they laughing? Or are they? Or is it the *Second Law of Nature (re: Levitation)* according to which: When you levitate, the sky is always blue and the sun is always shining, and no sound disturbs you. And indeed, no sound is disturbing him, the sun is shining, the sky is blue. He sniffs the air. He sniffs again, and his nose detects a whiff of roasted meat. He smiles. Oh well, so that's what they are waiting for: the Barbecue! He smiles again, but . . . But what on earth! But how can that be? Didn't Mrs Shepherd tell him that the Island was vegetarian? All animals forbidden. No animals allowed. Whom are they barbecueing?

He stopped abruptly, suspended in the middle of the air. Why did he say *Whom*? Whom are they barbecueing? Whom are they putting a spit through and roasting whole? He has an awful feeling that this is a question the answer to which he already knew long ago. He doesn't want to think about it. But the smell of roasted meat comes to him from somewhere there,

below,

from under the trees;

he doesn't want to know, but he does know that there, hidden under the green foliage of the heads of the trees, stands an iron framework, on which, turning round, is barbecued, whole, Academician Sakharov who has developed a hydrogen bomb;

or is it Dr Louis Fieser who's managed to mix naphthalene with coconut and make napalm bombs;

or is it his own son, Adam, Sir Adam D'Earth, who invented monkeys that make you die of laughter?

•

He flutters nervously in the breeze but he doesn't descend to see the Barbecue Machine. He knows the danger. He knows the *Ultimate Law of Nature (re: Levitation)* which says: If, when levitating, you lower yourself to touch the Earth or anything that is fixed to it or grows on it, Gravity will take over and everything will start from the beginning. He knows that once upon a time there was a footnote explaining the meaning of the word 'Beginning', but the footnote was lost in the river of time, and he wouldn't now dare to run the risk of touching even the topmost leaf of the highest tree.

He climbs up another 200 feet, and another.

Damn Adam!

He loops the loop high above the Island, and he smiles. This is a laughable world, but God has got a finger in it, and has created cruelty and pain and injustice so that you would stop laughing when life tickles your armpits or your brain. But one can always smile. And especially when one levitates.

God or no God
Fieser or no Fieser
Sakharov or no Sakharov
Adam or no Adam,

He smiles, and the smile takes him gently higher and higher up towards the blue sky and the shining sun. What a pity, he thinks, that God didn't smile when He created the world,

and Jesus didn't smile,

and Marx didn't smile,

nor did Lenin,

and economists do not smile, and how can he, who used to be stockbroker, how can he take them seriously if there is no symbol for a smile in all the equations they produce?

The gentle smile that costs you nothing to give and means so much when you receive it.

The sky is blue and the sun is shining and he has just made the most important discovery.

His mind has just produced the most important thought.

What a pity he can't find the words to express it. The word

'smile' is in it, but otherwise . . . it is just a thought, it may not even be true, but it is a lovely thought, and all lovely thoughts have a right to exist, perhaps for ever and ever, even if not true, even if there are no words to express them, and he loops another loop under the blue sky, under the shining sun,

    and now the thought has changed into colour,

    and the colour has changed into sound,

    and the sound has changed into silence.

## ABOUT THE AUTHOR

Stefan Themerson (1910-1988) was born in Poland, moved to Russia during the Revolution, studied physics and architecture in Warsaw, and lived in Paris before settling in London. Aside from his writings—which include novels such as *Tom Harris*, *The Mystery of the Sardine*, and *Professor Mmaa's Lecture*, children's stories, philosophical essays, and poems—Themerson also composed music and made a number of films with his wife Franciszka.

## SELECTED DALKEY ARCHIVE PAPERBACKS

**FOR A FULL LIST OF PUBLICATIONS, VISIT:**
www.dalkeyarchive.com

# SELECTED DALKEY ARCHIVE PAPERBACKS

**FOR A FULL LIST OF PUBLICATIONS, VISIT:**
www.dalkeyarchive.com